Soon

MORRIS GLEITZMAN

PUFFIN

PUFFIN BOOKS

UK | USA | Canada | Ireland | Australia
India | New Zealand | South Africa

Puffin Books is part of the Penguin Random House group of companies
whose addresses can be found at global.penguinrandomhouse.com.

puffinbooks.com

First published in Australia by Penguin Group (Australia) 2015
First published in Great Britain by Puffin Books 2015
007

Text copyright © Morris Gleitzman, 2015

The moral right of the author has been asserted

Set in 13/15.5 Minion by Post Pre-Press Group, Brisbane, Queensland
Printed and bound in Great Britain by Clays Ltd, Elcograf S.p.A.

A CIP catalogue record for this book is available from the British Library

ISBN: 978-0-141-36279-3

www.greenpenguin.co.uk

MIX
Paper from
responsible sources
FSC® C018179

Penguin Random House is committed to a
sustainable future for our business, our readers
and our planet. This book is made from Forest
Stewardship Council® certified paper.

For the children who had no hope

Soon, I hope, the world will be a safe and happy place.

This morning it isn't.

Over there, for example. On the roof of the apartment building next door.

Two of them. Or is it three? I can't see them because we've got sacks covering our windows, but I can hear their voices.

I try to keep my voice as quiet as I can.

'Gabriek,' I whisper urgently, 'Wake up.'

Gabriek mumbles but stays asleep.

I wish I didn't have to disturb him. When he hears what I'm hearing, his poor middle-aged heart valves might not make it through to breakfast.

My heart valves are hammering away like the engines on a plummeting Nazi fighter plane.

You know how when a war ends and you give a big sigh because you've survived and things will be better and you start trying to live a normal daily life but things aren't better because the city has been wrecked and people are hungry so you lay low on the second floor and pray that intruders won't barge into your secret hideout and take it and kill you but now it looks like they're going to?

That's happening to me and Gabriek.

I slide out of bed and crouch low and wriggle over to the window. I open the sack curtains a bit and wipe my glasses and peer through the cracked windowpanes at the roof next door.

The dawn light is murky, but I can see them.

Three people.

They haven't seen us yet. They're not pointing and plotting. But they could at any moment. If they see our cabbages and parsley they won't be able to control themselves.

This is exactly what we said, me and Gabriek, when we found this place. Perfect except for one thing. The roof next door. The one spot we can be seen from. But the building under it is so wrecked we didn't think anyone would make it up there.

This lot have.

They must be desperate.

I know how they feel. Me and Gabriek have to move fast to save ourselves.

I wriggle back to Gabriek's bed.

'Gabriek,' I say more loudly. 'Wake up.'

While I shake him I look around the hideout, trying to decide what we can take with us.

The vegetable gardens in the oil drums are too heavy. The firewood is mostly still furniture and we haven't got time to smash it up. The pickled cabbage? Gabriek's vodka-making equipment? My medical library? Lucky I've only got two books.

Gabriek sits up.

'What's going on?' he mumbles groggily.

He's a very heavy sleeper. People who drink a lot of alcohol usually are.

'The roof next door,' I say. 'Three adults.'

I hurry back to the window to see if they're heading this way.

That's strange. Something about these people doesn't look right. It's the way they're standing. They don't look like ruthless violent home-stealers. They look scared. Like fugitives.

Then I see something else.

Creeping up behind the people, ducking between broken roof beams and collapsed chimneys, are several men.

With guns.

The people haven't seen the men.

Suddenly I know who the people are, and the men. I bang on the window and yell.

'Look out.'

I only yell it once and I don't manage to get a window open to warn the people because Gabriek, who isn't groggy any more, flings himself at me and we both thud to the floor.

'Felix,' he hisses. 'Are you crazy?'

Yelling out loud around here is a serious breach of security.

'Sorry,' I say.

But part of me isn't sorry. The war's over. This is meant to be peacetime. People shouldn't be shot in peacetime.

Too late.

Gunshots echo through the empty shattered buildings.

I kneel up and see the armed men throwing bodies down into the street.

Oh.

Gabriek drags me back onto the floor.

'How many times do I have to tell you,' he growls. 'One simple rule. Stay quiet and out of sight.'

Gabriek likes simple rules. Mostly I obey them because he's such a kind and generous friend and he's forty-two and I'm only thirteen and he knows how to keep us safe.

But I know things too.

I know exactly who those murdering thugs are. I don't even need to see the badges on their leather jackets.

Poland For The Poles, the badges say.

'Those selfish bullies aren't interested in us,' I say to Gabriek. 'They're just after people who aren't Polish.'

Gabriek gives me a look.

'We're warm here,' he says, 'and we're dry and we've got food. Everybody's interested in that. So

4

we don't want anyone knowing about this place, specially brutal killers.'

Gabriek's right. But that doesn't stop me wishing I could have helped those poor dead people lying in the street. Hunted down just because they were in the wrong country when the war ended.

'Somebody should tell certain vicious pustules the war's over,' I mutter. 'Tell them to stop killing and try a bit of sharing.'

'Listen to me,' says Gabriek, his mouth very close to my ear. And my nose, which a person shouldn't do when they drink a lot of cabbage vodka.

'I'm listening,' I say, sliding away a bit.

'You want to change the world,' says Gabriek. 'That's natural at your age. But only dreamers try to change things when the world's in this state. Sensible people know it's as much as we can do to look after ourselves.'

I don't argue.

I know how lucky we are, surviving this long. How lucky I am to have Gabriek's good protection.

'How do you spot a sensible person?' says Gabriek.

I sigh. Gabriek says this at least once a day.

'They're alive,' says Gabriek. 'Sensible people stay alive because they don't get involved in other people's business and they don't take risks.'

I keep my mouth shut. Partly because it's what sensible people do when they're lying on a floor that always has rat poo on it no matter how often you sweep. But mostly because Gabriek wouldn't want to hear what I'm thinking.

I'm thinking of all the people who got involved in my business.

Who took risks for me.

Barney and Genia and Zelda and the others.

OK, Gabriek's right. They're not here. They can't be. They're dead.

But I'm here because of them, and the best way I can thank them is to be like them.

Soon, I hope, people won't have to creep out of their homes each morning like I'm doing now.

Tense.

Anxious.

Scared of being seen.

I poke my head out into the street and look both ways like Gabriek taught me.

Good. It's raining. Not many people around. Nobody being shot.

Yet.

Before I slip away, I listen carefully, trying to hear Gabriek snoring two floors above. I can't, but I know he is. That's good too. My ears were trained by partisans, so if I can't hear him, nobody can.

I hurry away through the rubble, hood up, head down, not stopping till I get into an alley.

I like alleys. They're narrow and secret and you find interesting things in them. They smell a bit because of the dead bodies from the war under the rubble, but you can get anywhere in the city through alleys as long as they're not blocked by bits of buildings or crashed planes.

And mostly you can do it without being seen. It's better to move around in secret if possible. It's safer, and it's harder for people to kill you.

They still try sometimes.

Gabriek would definitely try to kill me if he knew where I was going.

'Excuse me,' I say to an elderly woman. 'Can I help with that?'

The woman is sitting on the kerb, hunched over and sobbing. The crowd swirling around us in the square is ignoring her. One of the woman's fingers is sticking out from her hand at a medically very painful angle.

This city square is a war zone. It's the same every time there's a food drop.

You'd think experienced international charity relief organisations would know by now that when they hand out food, thousands of hungry people are going to fight and squabble for it.

The elderly woman gives me a suspicious glare through her tears.

I see why. Under her coat, gripped tight in her other hand, is a lump of bread.

'It's OK,' I say, crouching down and touching her arm gently. 'I'm a doctor.'

That's not really true. I won't be one for years.

But I have to say that. Members of the public can't just go around doing medical stuff.

I take a small piece of wood out of my medical bag, which I keep hidden under my coat. It's actually an old flour sack, but it's all I've got for now.

I kneel in front of the elderly woman and put the wood between her gums.

'Bite on this,' I say. 'It's been boiled.'

I take a deep breath to steady my hands. I've only done this treatment once before, and that time I had some help. There were two partisans holding the patient down.

I crack the woman's finger back into place.

She screams. The piece of wood flies out of her mouth and hits me in the head.

'Sorry,' I say.

She holds her injured finger and wails.

'Let me put a splint on that,' I say. 'It won't hurt so much with a splint.'

The elderly woman kicks me between the legs. The pain makes my head flop forward onto the cobbles.

Gabriek would probably say, I told you so. But I don't care. When you're educating yourself to be a doctor, you need all the practice you can get.

'Now, now,' says a voice. 'Be a good patient. The doctor's only trying to help you.'

I look up. My eyes are watering and at first I can't see clearly who spoke. I blink a few times so I can.

A girl. She's a bit older than me and she's wearing

a grubby pink coat. She's holding something black against the elderly woman's head.

I blink again.

It's a gun.

The elderly woman is stiff with fear.

'She's ready for the splint now,' says the girl.

My hands are fumbling as I take two more pieces of wood and a bandage from my medical bag. I place the pieces of wood on each side of the woman's finger and bind it tightly with the bandage.

The woman is very brave. She doesn't make a sound. I think she might be in shock.

'All done,' says the girl, lowering the gun. 'Except for payment.'

She reaches inside the elderly woman's coat and takes the lump of bread. The woman doesn't say anything or try to stop her. Just stares at the gun. I don't say anything or try to stop her either. I'm staring at the gun too.

It's pointing at me now.

'This isn't fairyland,' says the girl.

'Sorry?' I say.

'Once upon a time,' says the girl, 'people were kind and generous. The whole day long. But things have changed.'

I still don't understand.

'This is 1945,' she says. 'You carrying on like this, being kind for free, you're taking bread out of other people's mouths. Keep on doing it, Doctor, and your fairy story will have a very medically sad ending.'

She taps me on the head with the barrel of her pistol.

'Understand?'

I nod. She's saying me helping people with their health is stopping other people earning a living.

But who? Splint manufacturers? Undertakers? People who amputate fingers for cash?

Her?

I don't ask.

The girl puts the gun into her coat pocket and walks off into the crowd, the bread under her arm.

Me and the elderly woman look at each other.

'Sorry,' I say.

The elderly woman scowls and walks away. She looks like she wishes she'd kicked me harder.

I don't think I was a very good doctor just then. In one of my medical books it says how a doctor should try to make a patient feel relaxed and safe. I don't think that patient felt relaxed and safe, even before the girl arrived with the gun.

I turn to leave.

The crowd in the square is thinning out. The people with food are scurrying away. The people without food are trying to stop them. It's not working because mostly the people with the food are bigger and stronger.

Which is how the world is these days.

I think of Zelda. If she hadn't died three years ago, would she be like that girl? Tough and violent and greedy?

I don't think so.

Zelda was only six, but you should have seen her loving heart. I know what Zelda would have said.

That girl's not the boss of this square. The pigeons are. Doesn't she know anything?

Thinking of Zelda makes me smile. Even though most of the pigeons have been eaten.

Suddenly the day doesn't seem so bad.

But only for a moment.

'You!'

I look up.

A man is shouting at me as he comes towards me.

I step back.

He's huge and he looks very angry.

Before I can duck away, he grabs me by the neck and lifts me off the ground.

For a second I think he must be a relative of the elderly woman, come to complain about the standard of her medical treatment.

Then I see an older man standing next to him, and I see the door-lock the older man is carrying, and I know it's much more serious than that.

Soon, I hope, the man will put me down.

But I'll still be in trouble.

He's very big and very furious. The older man with him holding the lock is smaller, but he's doing a lot of scowling too.

The people crossing the city square aren't going to save me. They aren't even looking at me. People around here always look at the ground to stay out of trouble and so they won't trip over bits of buildings and unexploded bombs.

'Where's your father?' the big man is yelling at me. 'Your thieving cheating father.'

He doesn't mean my real father, who is dead and never cheated anybody. He means Gabriek, who never cheated anybody either.

I'm starting to go dizzy. The man's huge hand is still clamped round my throat and I can't get any words out. Or hardly any air in.

I look pleadingly at the people hurrying past.

'Where is he?' yells the man again.

Even if I could croak it out I wouldn't tell them. Gabriek goes back to bed most mornings till his head stops hurting from the cabbage vodka. It makes him sound unreliable, but he's not.

'Put the boy down, Dimmi,' says the older man. 'If you break his neck we won't get our lock mended.'

'Dad,' says Dimmi. 'Let me do this.'

The older man gives him a stern look.

Dimmi glares at me as if breaking my neck is tempting. But he puts me down.

I gasp some breaths.

My head feels wobbly and I'm finding it hard to think straight. But I know the big lock Dimmi's father is holding is one of ours. Well, I found it and Gabriek fixed it up, which made it ours.

'Good pork fat we paid,' says Dimmi. 'Good pork fat for a quality lock. Quality lock, pah.'

He spits on my boots.

'It is a quality lock,' I say. 'Off a castle.'

I'm not sure if that's completely true. I got it off the door of a pickle factory. But it's big, so it could have come from a castle originally.

'Look at it,' says Dimmi. 'Two days, broken.'

His eyes are like angry embers set deep in his big fleshy head. They're burning so brightly it's a wonder his beard doesn't burst into flames.

He grabs my chin with a hand that's got more meat on it than I've seen on a dinner table since I was four.

I have a thought a doctor shouldn't have. The rumour is that over in Silesia, people are eating each other. Dimmi wouldn't last a week there.

'Let me get it looked at,' I say, reaching for the lock. 'All our work is guaranteed.'

That's true, it is. Gabriek insists on it. Which is pretty generous when your business is fixing up stuff that's been bombed.

Dimmi's father hands me the lock, and the key we made for it.

'Let the boy go,' he says to Dimmi. 'It's guaranteed. The quicker we get it mended, the better.'

Dimmi gives a big angry sigh and puts his face closer to mine.

'Here's my guarantee,' he says. 'If that lock's not mended by tomorrow, I'll kill you and your father.'

Dimmi's father doesn't say anything.

I nod to show them I've got the message.

Dimmi doesn't know where we live, but he knows we can't stay off the streets for ever.

In the good old days, when I was a little kid, nobody would kill two people over a lock. But the bossy girl was right. Times have changed.

I'm hoping one day they'll change back. And I want me and Gabriek to be around when they do.

So I hope this lock can be mended.

Gabriek, please, don't drink too much this morning.

* * *

15

I don't like going home in daylight like this.

Darkness is safer. People can't see where you're heading. And if you're being followed it's easier to give people the slip in the dark.

But this is an emergency.

With a bit of luck I'll be home before Gabriek has his breakfast vodka. So he can fix the lock. Get Dimmi off our necks.

All this fuss over a simple repair.

Why couldn't Dimmi and his dad have just said to themselves, poor Gabriek, when he worked on this lock he was probably sad from missing his dear dead wife and probably drank too much vodka and overlooked a bit of bomb damage. Easily fixed. No need to make a big fuss with violent threats and oxygen deprivation.

But no.

Which is typical of how things are these days. People's friendliness and manners are as wrecked as these streets.

What's that noise?

Gunshots.

That's exactly what I mean. I bet that's people losing their tempers over something stupid. A bit of one person's rubble falling into another person's soup or something.

Hang on, I don't think it is.

Those people running out of that building look like they're worried about something more serious than rubble in their turnip broth.

Oh.

That boy's fallen over. He's not moving.

The running people are leaving him behind.

I look around. I can't see the people doing the shooting. They must be going another sneaky way through the ruins to cut the running people off. It's a trick those *Poland For The Poles* thugs use a lot.

I hurry over to the boy.

He's lying on bits of a bombed bathroom that are scattered where a kitchen used to be. He's almost as pale as the pieces of tiles and the pieces of sink.

'It hurts,' he says in a small scared voice.

He's bleeding badly.

In the distance, more gunfire.

I give my glasses a quick clean so I can see what I'm doing. I hunt through the boy's clothes, trying to find where the blood's coming from. There's so much of it you'd think it was from everywhere. But that's not possible, not with the boy's coat still in one piece.

He looks about seven. His pulse is very faint.

I find the gunshot wound. It's in his thigh.

I wish Gabriek was here. Mostly so he could help me do a clean and heat. These ripped veins and arteries need burning shut with a hot blade.

I also wish Gabriek could see this. A little boy bleeding to death in someone's kitchen.

Would he still say don't get involved?

The bullet went in and out so there are two

wounds and I have to stop the bleeding fast and I don't have time to make a fire myself.

Think about what you can do, Gabriek always says, not about what you can't.

I grab a bandage from my medical bag, and the disinfectant bottle and my scalpel. I cut the boy's trousers and pull the cloth away from the wounds.

The boy doesn't move or make a sound. I think he's gone unconscious.

I cut the trousers more, a long strip of cloth which I wind round the boy's leg above the bullet holes. I knot it as tightly as I can. Then I pour disinfectant onto the wounds.

The boy doesn't open his eyes or yell. This isn't good. The disinfectant is cabbage vodka, which hurts a lot.

I bandage the wounds as tightly as I can.

Blood comes through.

I've only got one bandage left. I cut another strip off the boy's trousers, wrap that over the wounds, then tie the last bandage on top.

Blood still comes through.

'I'm sorry,' I say.

It comes out almost as a sob, which is not how doctors should talk. But I can't help it. The boy still hasn't opened his eyes.

'Don't upset yourself,' says a gruff voice.

I look up.

A man is standing over me. He's looped with ammunition belts and is holding a machine gun.

Two other armed men are behind him.

They've all got *Poland For The Poles* badges on their jackets.

'Time to move on,' says the first man. 'Next patient's waiting.'

He grabs me with one hand and yanks me up.

'No,' I yell, trying to get back to the boy. 'I haven't finished.'

The man pulls me further away.

'You did your best,' he says. 'That's all anyone can do. And it's more than a Fritz deserves.'

He shoots the boy.

I scream and hurl myself at the man, trying to rip his eyes, his lips, anything.

The other two men grab me and slap me and a sack is jammed over my head. I'm flung over what feels like someone's shoulder and my ankles are gripped so tightly all I can think about is the pain.

Which is a relief.

That's the good thing about pain.

It helps you when you can't bear to think about other things.

Soon, I hope, I'll know where these *Poland For The Poles* thugs are taking me.

Wherever it is, we're going there by truck. I can hear the engine howling and whining through the sack over my head, and I can feel the metal floor shuddering under me.

We bump along some streets.

Fast, it feels like.

I start thinking about the boy. An innocent kid, shot by grown-ups he didn't even know.

Barney and Genia and Zelda would be so disappointed if they knew the war was over and people were still doing that.

We stop.

I'm lifted down from the truck.

Well, dropped. Which isn't good for legs like mine. I still get leg pain after the two years I spent hiding in a hole. But I'm not letting these pustules know that.

The sack is pulled off. I blink in the daylight.
We're in a courtyard, me and about ten armed men.

One of them comes over to me.

Stares at me.

Snorts.

Swears at the other men.

'I said a doctor,' he hisses.

The other men glance at each other.

'At the food drop they say he's good,' says the
one who shot the wounded boy.

The snorter, who must be the leader from the
way the other men aren't shooting him for being
rude, snorts again.

'He's a child,' he scowls.

'I'm a surgical assistant,' I say indignantly. 'Six
months with Doctor Zajak in a partisan unit in the
forest.'

I don't know why I said that. There's no way I'm
offering my services to these murderers.

The leader gives me another hard stare. He's not
very old, but he's going bald. His wispy pale hair
looks like it's trying to get as far away as it can from
his angry face.

I try to stare back.

'Bring him,' snaps the leader to the other men.

They take me into a room off the courtyard.
Lying on a table is a wounded man, whimpering.
He's got a broken leg. I don't need to be an expert
on bones to know that. I can see them sticking out
of his thigh.

He's bleeding badly. The men feeding him vodka aren't doing a very good job of stopping the blood.

'Do what you have to,' says the leader to me.

One of the other men pushes my medical bag into my hands.

I hesitate.

My medical books say a doctor's job is to care for human life. To heal everyone. To do no harm.

This man is in agony. His human life will be over if he bleeds much more. But if I stop the bleeding, what harm will he do when he's back on his feet?

I need a book about difficult medical decisions.

I haven't got one.

The thug leader helps out.

'If he lives,' says the leader, 'then you live.'

I decide to accept the offer. Most people would. It just means that in the future I'll have to do a lot of good things to make up for whatever the man on the table does.

The leader goes.

I get my scalpels out of my medical bag. At least Dimmi's lock is still there.

While the men get the other things I need for a clean and heat, I try to stop my hands shaking.

I've never done a medical job this big before, not without Doctor Zajak to help me. What if I can't do it? Doctor Zajak was very grumpy, but he never actually shot me if I got something wrong.

A couple of the men jam a leather gun holster into the wounded man's mouth for him to bite on.

One of the others heats a scalpel blade.

About six of them hold the man down.

I splash vodka over his leg. I try to ignore his yells and sort out his blood vessels as best I can. Carefully, I sear the damaged ones closed. The man makes a lot of noise. I know he's a killer, but I feel sorry for him because there's worse to come.

'This might hurt a bit,' I tell him, which I think is the professional thing to say, but I don't know if it's actually going to help much.

I climb up onto the table. I take a deep breath. Using all my body weight and as much of Doctor Zajak's knowledge as I can remember, I push the man's bones back into place.

Sort of.

It's the best I can do without plaster and a bone diagram book. He'll live if he doesn't rupture his throat with all the screaming. But he'll be a cripple. Which isn't all bad. It might give his victims the chance to run away.

My arms have gone weak with the stress and the responsibility. It takes me a while to bandage the man's leg with boiled sheet strips.

'You're good,' says one of the other men. 'We thought we'd lost him. He fell down a lift shaft chasing a Jew.'

I don't ask what happened to the poor Jewish person. I'm just glad they don't know I'm one.

The men slap me on the back very hard and toast me in vodka. Then one nudges the others.

'Gogol,' he hisses.

They finish their vodka quickly.

The leader comes back in. He looks at the patient's bandage and nods.

'Are you a patriot?' he says.

I realise Gogol is talking to me.

I hesitate. I'm not sure exactly what a patriot is. I think it's somebody who kills other people for not being patriots.

'Let's see if you are,' says Gogol. 'Bring him.'

A couple of the men grab me.

I've got a horrible feeling there's worse to come for me too.

We're back on the truck.

They kept me locked up for a few hours, and now we're driving around. I'm sitting in the front between Gogol and the driver. My head's not in a sack this time so I can see where we're going.

Streets.

Wrecked streets, empty and dark.

'Our beautiful country,' says Gogol, staring out at the broken buildings as we lurch and thump between them.

Is this the patriot test? I want to do well in the patriot test. If I do well, I'm hoping they won't shoot me before I can get away.

But I'm not sure what to say.

Our country isn't beautiful at the moment.

When I was a little kid, me and Dad used to

build cities out of breadcrumbs on the table after dinner. Beautiful cities. One time Mum accidentally opened the window and an entire city vanished. Just breadcrumbs blowing in the breeze.

That's what happened to our country.

Except it wasn't a breeze.

'Our great and glorious nation,' says Gogol. 'Crawling with vermin.'

I try to look like I agree.

'Nazis?' I say.

Gogol scowls and spits out the truck window.

'Forget the Nazis,' he says. 'Poland has been crawling with vermin for centuries. Germans, Austrians, Jews, Ukrainians, Russians. Now we're cleaning them up.'

I hate it when people say things like that. Cleaning up is what you do to rubble blocking the street and rat poo on the floor. Cleaning up isn't killing people.

I'm not sure if it's patriotic to tell somebody a thing they might not know, but I'm going to anyway.

'That wounded boy your men shot today,' I say. 'He wasn't foreign, he was Polish.'

Gogol glares at me like he's starting to think I might be vermin myself.

I stick my jaw out to make me look like a tough Polish patriot, and try to explain.

'He spoke without a foreign accent,' I say. 'So he was born here.'

'Of course he was born here,' sneers Gogol. 'That's the problem. Outsiders have been spawning in our belly for centuries. When I shot his parents, and the slimy parasites begged for mercy, you could have sharpened a knife on their accents.'

I don't think I'm going to pass the patriot test. If it goes on much longer, I think I'm going to fail it for being sickened by the testing person and bashing him on the head with a large lock.

'Over there,' yells a voice in the back of the truck. 'Apes.'

The driver stops the truck with a skid.

Gogol's men leap out.

In a nearby building, lights are flickering and the shadows of people are moving.

'I've been after this pack for a long time,' mutters Gogol.

He turns to me.

'Wait here,' he says. 'Some of these vermin bite. Likely be more work for you tonight.'

Gogol jumps down from the truck and turns to me again.

'Don't think of running,' he says. 'You're only alive because you're useful. If you run, I'll find you.'

He goes.

'He will,' says the driver, clambering out of the truck. 'One morning you'll wake up and smell bacon and he'll be there, sitting on the end of your bed with a frying pan, cooking your feet.'

The driver goes too.

Gunshots and screams echo inside the building. I don't know what to do.

I want to go inside and care for human life. But I also want to care for my own human life, and disobeying somebody like Gogol feels like a very unwise medical decision.

That's something else I don't like about being thirteen. You're not a kid any more, but you still get scared.

Doesn't matter. You can still do things when you're scared. I've seen partisan fighters hold off a whole Nazi tank while they were scared rigid and their urinary tracts weren't coping that well either.

I'm going in there.

I open the truck door and jump down. And almost land on top of somebody. My heart valves lock. Gogol must have left a guard to shoot me if I try to get away.

I tense all my muscles to run. But the person staring at me isn't a selfish bully or a demented patriot or a murdering thug.

It's a scared woman.

She looks as terrified as me. Her arms are wrapped round a cloth parcel. She holds it out.

'Please,' she says, with a strong accent. 'Please.'

She pushes the parcel into my arms.

Before I can say anything she runs away. But she's running in the wrong direction. Back towards the building. There must be somebody or something in there that's very important to her.

Except what she's doing is suicide.

Gogol's men are coming out of the building. They start shooting. The woman weaves to one side, then the other.

Bullets hit her.

She spins and falls. Twists in agony on the ground. Shudders, then goes still.

I'm not staying still. I crouch low and head off in the opposite direction. My legs, which get even more stiff and painful when they're scared, don't make it easy. Running might be suicide for me too, but I'm not staying here. I'm not patching up another vicious killer ever and I don't care if that makes me selfish or a bad doctor or both.

Gabriek's been right all along. We should just take care of ourselves.

Don't get involved.

Don't take risks.

I reach a bombed-out building and clamber in through a hole in the wall and squat panting under what used to be a desk.

My chest hurts, mostly for the dead woman, but also because I'm so out of breath.

I realise I'm still holding the woman's parcel.

No wonder I'm out of breath. It's heavy. But I'm panting so hard the parcel feels like it's moving.

Wait a sec, it is moving.

Something's wriggling inside it.

Part of me wants to throw the parcel away and keep running. But I don't. I start unwrapping it.

I've heard about this. People who love their pets so much they'll do anything to save them.

I can't leave a living creature to starve.

This must be a puppy. No way a cat would stay wrapped up like this.

I loosen the last layer, which is a tiny ragged blanket.

Suddenly there's loud howling.

A small face is staring up at me, jaws open, furious. For a second I'm stunned. Then I put my hand over its mouth to try to smother the sound.

It's not a dog, it's a baby.

Soon, I hope, you'll be safe, baby boy.

Or girl.

I haven't had time to check. Sorry about that, I've been too busy keeping an eye out for Gogol and his lot. And doing these sudden turns behind piles of rubble, which I always do to throw people off the scent on my way home.

But mostly I've been worrying what Gabriek will do when I turn up with you.

It'll probably be OK. It's only for one night. Gabriek has lots of customers so we'll find someone to look after you, little bundle.

This dark's a bit scary, eh?

Don't worry, I know these streets. And my eyes are good in the dark. Gabriek spent six clocks on these new glasses for me, so we'll be fine.

As long as you don't cry. Please don't cry. We're never sure who's lurking in these buildings, and nothing attracts strangers like a crying baby.

I know you're probably hungry, little bundle. Gabriek and me will make you dinner. It won't be milk, but it'll be something you'll like. Turnip juice tastes a bit like milk if you add pork fat.

Hear that? Loud, eh? Don't be startled, it's just a wardrobe door banging in the wind.

You probably don't even know this, but before you were born, wardrobe doors hardly ever banged in the wind because all the buildings had walls.

Yeah, I know, hard to believe.

Me and Gabriek are lucky, our place has mostly got them.

Here we are.

Good, isn't it? You wouldn't know anyone was up there, would you? It's because we've got sack curtains with tar painted on the inside, which is one of Gabriek's security inventions. It's a brilliant idea and the smell's not that bad really.

I know what you're probably thinking. How will we get ourselves up through this big gaping empty bomb space between the ground floor and the second floor?

Watch.

See? An automatic folding ladder. Just tug on this hidden rope and down it comes.

Gabriek made it. All from just forty-eight door hinges, sixteen wrecked dining chairs, two pulleys from a bombed-out beer factory and a hook from a dead slaughterhouse.

Not bad for someone who drinks a lot, is it?

At the top, after I've pulled the ladder up, I'll do a secret knock on the door. It's my name in a code only Gabriek and I know.

It's another one of Gabriek's security inventions. They're his favourite kind of invention these days.

Security means keeping people out, little bundle.

Which is why I'm a bit worried about what he'll do. After a long day's scavenging I've often turned up with unusual things, but never anything like you.

Gabriek doesn't do anything.

Just stares.

I hold the bundle out so he can see it more clearly. No point trying to hide a baby.

From the expression on Gabriek's face I think he's having trouble taking it all in. He opens and closes his mouth a few times, and rubs his hair, which he does when he's stunned.

'It's a baby,' I say.

'I know,' says Gabriek. 'I know it's a baby. Are you crazy? This is a hideout. You don't bring a crying baby into a hideout.'

'It's just for tonight,' I say. 'And she's not crying.'

I'm hoping it's a girl. Before the Nazis killed Genia, she and Gabriek always dreamed of having a daughter. Gabriek might relax if it's a girl.

'Her parents are dead,' I say.

I tell Gabriek about the woman giving me the bundle and getting shot. I don't tell him about Gogol and me. No point getting him worried.

Gogol would have been furious when he got back to the truck and found I'd run off, and it's never good to have a vicious murdering thug furious with you.

Gabriek sits down. I'm not sure if it's emotion or vodka.

'We'll find somebody tomorrow,' I say. 'To look after her. Somebody who owes you a favour for fixing their bike or something.'

Gabriek takes a deep breath. The one he does when he's very cross.

'It's a simple rule,' he says, using the quiet angry voice we have to use here because we can't shout. 'No visitors.'

'She's not a visitor,' I reply in my quiet angry voice. 'She's a patient. If I'd left her behind, she wouldn't have survived medically.'

'You've put us at risk,' says Gabriek.

'How?' I say.

Gabriek throws his arms up, exasperated. I'm glad he's not holding his vodka mug.

'A crying baby,' he says.

'She's not crying,' I say, just as exasperated.

The baby, who obviously knows an argument when she hears it, even a quiet one, starts to cry.

At last.

I thought the tears would never stop.

Thank goodness for biscuit soup.

Gabriek let me use our last three army biscuits.

Those biscuits cost us a whole repaired bucket, so it was very kind of him. Specially as the baby had just peed on Gabriek's coat and we'd had the disappointment of discovering it's a boy.

Well, I was disappointed. Didn't seem to make any difference to Gabriek. He was just as grumpy about the baby as before.

Luckily it turns out babies really like biscuit soup. You have to remember to strain off the biscuit sludge before you give it to them. And a tiny splash of cabbage vodka in it helps too, specially getting them to sleep afterwards.

Gabriek and the baby are both asleep now. Gabriek in his bed and the baby in mine.

I'm fixing the lock myself.

Gabriek had a lot to put up with tonight so I didn't want to bother him with it. After the amount of vodka he drank he's fast asleep and won't notice the candle.

I'm glad I didn't tell Gabriek about the lock. Now I've got it in pieces, I can see it wasn't bomb damage that made it break. It was Gabriek. He put it back together wrong after we made the key. A mistake like that would be very distressing to a skilled craftsman like him.

'What are you doing?'

Gabriek's voice makes me jump so hard I almost drop the driver pins onto the floor, and we've got gaps between some of our floorboards big enough to lose turnips through.

I try to push the lock under my blanket.

Too late. Gabriek is standing over my bed, staring at it.

'It got sent back for repair,' I mumble.

'Why didn't you tell me?' he says.

I can see he's angry and hurt. I try to think of a way to save his feelings.

'I wanted to see if I could mend it,' I say.

Gabriek gives me a hard look. I'm not sure if he believes me.

Then he sighs and sits on my bed. He tries to do it carefully so he doesn't wake the baby, but he's unsteady on his feet and the bed lurches. My bed is pretty wobbly anyway. It's a big sack of sponges from a bombed-out chemist shop.

The baby gives a whimper.

I stroke its head.

'I know why you didn't tell me,' says Gabriek quietly.

I wait for him to say more.

He doesn't.

It must be hard when you're a grown-up, to admit you made a mistake because of vodka. I can see how ashamed Gabriek feels.

'We all make mistakes,' I say.

Gabriek looks at the baby for a few moments.

'In the morning,' he says, 'take it to the military authorities. Their welfare office, two blocks north of food-drop square. The military work with all the child charity agencies. Much better than trying to persuade one of my customers to take on another mouth to feed.'

I feel a pang of sadness at the thought of handing the baby over to somebody in an office. But I know Gabriek's right.

'Will you come?' I say.

Gabriek shakes his head.

'Better if you go on your own,' he says. 'This city is awash with orphan babies. They might take more pity on a kid.'

I nod. Even though I'm not technically a kid.

Gabriek reaches for his vodka mug and stares into it.

'Felix,' he says.

He pauses. I wait for him to finish what he wants to say.

'Thank you,' he says.

For a second I'm not sure why he's thanking me. Is it for not starting another argument about the baby?

Gabriek picks up the lock.

'It's not only these things that give people good protection,' he says quietly. 'Thanks for watching out for me.'

He gives me a long hug.

Thirteen is a bit old for that, but the war's only been over a few months so things aren't back to normal yet.

As we finish the hug, I feel a stab of guilt. I still haven't told Gabriek about Gogol.

I'm tempted to tell him now, but I don't.

Gabriek would insist on coming with me in the morning, and that could muck things up at the welfare office.

It's not fair to put this baby's future at risk just because I'm feeling a bit nervous about my own good protection.

I'll be extra careful.

Gogol won't see us.

We'll be fine.

Soon, I hope, I'll get this little baby safely to the military welfare office and we can both relax.

This trip is stressful for both of us.

I've got my hood up and my head down in case Gogol's men are on the streets. So I'm having to be extra careful not to bump into people or fall into bomb craters.

The baby's inside my coat for security, but I'm worried he might be getting too hot.

Sorry, little bundle.

I wish we were in an alley. We're taking this rubble-cleared street for speed, but in an alley it'd be safer to give you a breath of fresh air.

I lift him out of my coat anyway.

There, that's better, little bundle.

No, it's not.

A truck roars towards us. I turn to run. My boots slide on wet brick-dust and I half slip over. I hold the baby tight in my arms and brace myself for bullets.

They don't come.

I sag with relief. I can see now it's not Gogol, it's an army truck. Followed by more army trucks. A convoy of them.

I duck down against a wall.

I don't really have to, this isn't the Nazi army. The Nazis are mostly all dead or in prison camps. These are American or English or Russian soldiers. But you still stay away from them. It's safer. Soldiers can search you whenever they like, and sometimes they take you off to displaced persons camps where they think you'll be happier.

You won't.

The convoy stops. So do my heart valves.

I tense myself again to run, careful of the brick-dust this time.

Then I see why the trucks have stopped. Kids' toys have been piled up, blocking the street. It's an old trick. Gangs who want to stop army trucks hope soldiers won't drive over little kids' toys.

This convoy has fallen for it.

There's the gang, older kids, swarming over the back of a food truck.

Soldiers rushing to stop them.

That's another part of the trick. Soldiers always think gangs want food. So they concentrate on trying to keep the kids off the food trucks. They forget there's something they've got that's even more precious than food.

Over there is the real point of all this.

At the side of that truck at the back of the convoy. Somebody kneeling down with a rubber tube, syphoning petrol into a big can.

Somebody wearing a dirty pink coat.

I stare.

She looks up. Straight at me.

Her face is as unfriendly as last time. But sort of curious too. She's probably wondering why I'm carrying a baby.

I don't hang around to explain. I duck into an alley and get out of there as fast as I can.

That girl is one person I don't want to get involved with.

The baby starts crying.

I know, little bundle, it must be scary, rushing along an alley with someone who's not your mum or dad. And being scared can make you very thirsty, it's a medical fact.

We'll have to risk a drink stop.

Just a quick one.

I climb down into the cellar of a wrecked building, away from the eyes of violent patriots and angry customers and unfriendly girls.

The drink bottle I've got doesn't have a proper baby teat, but the baby doesn't mind. He gobbles the drops as fast as I plop them into his mouth.

It was good of Gabriek to make this sugar water, specially as he was saving the sugar for my birthday cake next year.

He's a very generous man, Gabriek, but I think he was also relieved to see the baby gone.

I won't be relieved to see the baby gone. I'm going to miss him.

I try not to think about that. While the baby drinks, I peer around for salvage opportunities, to say thank you to Gabriek.

It's mostly just typical house wreckage. Rubble, beams, pipes, bits of furniture, scraps of wallpaper, a small pile of poo from a previous visitor.

And a tap, lying on the ground, no pipes attached.

I pick it up. It's a bit rusty, but not too bad. I put it in my medical bag. Gabriek will be pleased. When the water comes back on, there'll be a big demand for taps in this city.

I rest the baby on a part of a settee, take out my notebook and scribble a note as usual.

> *Dear Tap-owner,*
> *Sorry I took your tap. But times are tough and it's as much as we can do to look after ourselves. When things improve I'll pay you back as soon as I can if you're still alive.*
> *In the meantime, try to eat vegetables if possible. They're quite important medically.*
> *Yours sincerely,*
> *Felix Salinger.*

Just because civilisation is in ruins, doesn't mean we can't be considerate of other people.

I tuck the note under a brick.

Then I see something half buried in the rubble.

Pages from a book. With diagrams of bodies on them. It looks like part of a medical book. I grab the pages. But the bodies aren't human, they're animals.

It's a cook book.

I'm not really surprised. Around here, medical books are scarcer than walls.

Ow.

What's that?

Biting me.

Tiny insects. All over me.

Oh no, and the baby.

Fleas.

Frantically I try to brush them off him, but there are more and more.

This cellar is alive with them.

I wrap my arms round the baby and scramble up into the building next door and straight through it and into the one on the other side.

This should be far enough away.

I tear the baby's bundle open, brushing as many fleas off his little body as I can, picking the last ones off with my fingernails, crushing them. I don't like doing it, they're just hungry like the rest of us, but you have to. Fleas can spread serious illness.

Then I lay the baby on my medical bag and wipe him over with cabbage vodka. He wriggles and yells from the smell and the stinging.

I explain to him why I'm doing it.

He doesn't look convinced.

Once he's safely bundled up, it's my turn.

I strip off and slap and crush and wipe.

'Haven't you got a bathroom of your own?' says a female voice behind me.

I'm so startled I almost drop the vodka bottle. I grab my trousers. Pull them on and turn round.

'Is that vodka?' says the girl, taking off her pink coat. 'Can I have a swig?'

'It's medicine,' I say.

Even if it wasn't, I wouldn't give her any. She's probably not even a year older than me.

I grab the baby and my medical bag. At least she hasn't got any of the boys from the gang with her.

The girl folds her coat and places it on a pile of rubble and sits on it. I don't know why she bothers. The yellow skirt she's wearing is even grubbier than the coat.

I want to ask her how she found me, but I don't really care. I just wish she hadn't.

'Nice baby,' she says, looking at the bundle. 'Yours?'

I don't say anything. I lay him down close to me while I put on my shirt and coat and scarf. I prefer not to chat with people who've threatened me with a gun. Particularly when they may also have seen my private part.

The girl gets up and comes over and looks more closely at the baby. She gives him a couple of gentle prods, as if she's never touched one before.

Suddenly I want to make it clear that this baby is not up for grabs. Or prods.

'He's going to America,' I say, picking him up. 'I'm helping him.'

The girl thinks about this.

'You're an unusual person,' she says.

I don't reply.

'We can use someone like you,' she says.

I stare at her.

'Interested?' she says.

I try to take this in. Is she asking me to join her gang? I think she is. I've never been asked to join a professional gang before. But I don't need to think about it for long.

'No, thanks,' I say.

'Why not?' she says.

I should just walk away. Somewhere in that coat she's got a gun. Never argue with someone who's got a gun, that's what Gabriek always says. Or is it an army?

Anyway, I don't walk away

'You took the old woman's bread,' I say.

The girl looks at me, frowning. I don't think she gets my point.

She's not a good person, but I can't help noticing the way her hair falls into her eyes. It's wavy and it's the colour that toast goes, sort of golden brown.

That's what I hate about being thirteen. Having so many parts of your body, including your eyes, that don't listen to your brain.

I snap out of it. For all I know her hair is blonde and the toast colour is just dirt.

'You've never been hungry, have you?' says the girl.

I look at her.

'Not really hungry,' she says.

I don't reply. She doesn't know anything about me.

'People who've been really hungry don't walk away from a lump of bread,' she says.

I walk away from her, telling my legs not to let me down. Wobbly legs can be embarrassing when you're trying to make a dignified exit.

The girl calls after me.

'Apart from the limp,' she says, 'you look to me like somebody who has a pretty good food supply. I'm guessing at home. So you're lucky. But luck doesn't last for ever. And that's when you need friends.'

I don't reply.

It's none of her business.

I've got friends. Good friends. Most of them just happen to be dead, that's all.

I keep walking.

Soon, I hope, all these people will get what they need and go home.

Before somebody gets hurt.

This welfare office is worse than food-drop square. There are just too many people, yelling and pleading and waving bits of paper and suitcases and babies in the air.

The officials at the counters look like their brains are hurting. Every time they start talking to one of the pleading people, someone else pushes in.

No wonder the officials are shouting a lot.

I'm not doing any baby-waving. My baby's too upset. I don't think he's seen human beings behaving like this before. He's probably thinking the same thing as me.

Everyone calm down.

Form a queue.

But we both know it's not that sort of world any more.

So far I haven't spoken to a single official. Not about America or Canada or anything. I haven't even got close enough to be shouted at. At this rate this poor little orphan will be an old-age pensioner before he starts his new life.

And I can feel his bundle getting soggy.

Come on, little one, I know your bladder's not very big, but make an effort. That's my blanket you're peeing on. I know you haven't experienced this yet, but other people's pee isn't very nice.

Wait a moment.

Brilliant idea.

Good thinking, little pensioner.

I clasp the baby tight to my chest and we push and wriggle our way through the crowd towards one of the military guards standing to attention in front of a doorway.

This is going to be risky, but I can't think of a better way.

I hold the baby low down in front of me so nobody can see what I'm doing. Luckily everybody's so frantic, they're not even looking.

I undo my trousers at the front.

I go up to the guard, who can't see what I'm doing either. I start peeing on the ground between his boots, making it look like the wee is leaking out of the bundle.

'Sorry,' I say to the guard. 'It's the sugar water. It goes through him like turnip juice. Is there a toilet, please?'

The guard takes a couple of moments to realise what's happening.

He yelps and jumps to one side, getting his boots splashed on the way.

With a painful effort I stop the flow. I read somewhere it's not medically advisable to do that, but sometimes you have to take a risk.

'Quick,' I say to the guard. 'A toilet. There's more coming.'

The guard looks around, flustered. Then he grabs me, opens the door and pushes me and the baby through.

'Be quick,' he snaps, before stepping back out and closing the door.

I'm in a long corridor. There's carpet all the way to the end and not a single bullet hole or pile of rubble anywhere. I'm impressed. When armies finish blowing things up, they do really good repairs.

Before me and the baby do what we're here for, I need to finish my pee.

I spot a door with a small silhouette of a man on it. The man is wearing a posh hat. I don't have a posh hat, but I go in anyway.

And stop. And stare.

The floor and walls are covered with gleaming white tiles. They go up twice as high as me. All around are sinks with no cracks. And taps with no rust. Peeing troughs, completely unstained, that are actually attached to the walls. Cubicles, each one with a door.

I've never seen anything like it.

Only the pain in my private part stops me gazing around for hours.

I lay the baby on a bench and finish my pee, sighing with relief. Then I unwrap him and use toilet paper, actual white toilet paper not boiled rags, to mop up some of the dampness.

His flea bites are coming up now, but there aren't as many as I'd feared and they don't seem to be bothering him too much. I wish I could say the same for mine.

I dab a bit of cabbage vodka on his, just to be sure. Pat him dry again with toilet paper.

'There,' I say to him, 'you're going to be fine now. You're going to be really well looked after here.'

The baby stops complaining about the vodka and chuckles.

He likes toilet paper. Who wouldn't? Most people have a choice between a roll of toilet paper or eating for a month.

I bundle him back up.

Suddenly I have a distant memory from when I was little. I leave the baby on the bench and go over to one of the sinks.

And turn the tap.

Water comes out. I stare at it. I let it splash over my fingers. I wonder if there's some way I could smuggle Gabriek in here, so we could all live here and never have to haul water up the ladder again.

I wash my hands. The soap smells wonderful.

It reminds me of Mum and Dad and makes me feel sad, but good.

I bring the baby over to the sink and gently wash his hands. So he'll have this memory too.

While I dry his hands he stares at me as if he's amazed. His eyes are even bigger than usual. His mouth is open and dribble is quivering on his lips. He's probably thinking what a strange world it is where a complete stranger will look after you.

'It's not,' I say to him. 'It's happened to me several times. And it's going to happen to you lots.'

I have a drink from the tap and give the baby more sugar water and tuck him under my arm and we go out to get him a happy future.

All the offices along the corridor are empty, except for one at the end.

A man in a very clean suit is sitting at a desk reading a piece of paper. His shirt is even whiter than the paper. If he took his jacket off and went into the toilet, he'd disappear.

I knock on the open door.

'Excuse me,' I say. 'This baby's parents are dead and he needs looking after. Is this the right department?'

I know it's a long shot. But Dad used to be a great believer in thinking positively.

The man stares at us.

'How did you get in here?' he says.

'Medical emergency,' I say. 'A urinary one.'

The man gives a little snort. A fairly friendly one, not like one of Gogol's.

'I need the department that looks after babies,' I say. 'The one that sends them to loving parents in America or Canada. Even somewhere like Alaska or Australia would be fine.'

The man smiles. But it's a sad smile.

'You and several million others,' he says.

That doesn't sound good, but perhaps the department is a big one.

'The repatriation people are totally swamped,' says the man. 'And I've got my hands full with other important projects. Finding long-term homes for Nazi war criminals, mostly. Very small homes with bars on the windows.'

I know he means jails, which is good news.

The bad news is he can't help us.

'Can you give us directions?' I say. 'To the right department?'

'Wouldn't be worth it,' says the man. 'You'd just be in queues for months and wasting your time. And you'd probably get hurt in the crowds. Go home. The young fella's better off with you.'

Desperately I try to think of something that will get my baby a bit of special treatment.

But I don't get the chance.

The military guard with the wet boots bursts in and grabs me.

Soon, I hope, my neck will stop hurting.

That military guard didn't have to be so rough. He could see I wasn't going to put up a fight. Not with a baby.

I squat down on the stone steps of the welfare office, hugging the baby in his bundle. It's a crowded place to sit. Hundreds of people are still churning around, lots of them carrying babies and children, all of them trying to get into the building, all desperate for help.

'No more fairy stories,' the guard said as he threw me out.

Rude pustule.

He knows this isn't a fairy story. He only has to look around.

I take a deep breath and try to calm down and think what to do now. I can't waste energy getting angry and calling people names.

The baby's gone very quiet.

'Are you OK?' I say, peeking into the bundle.

He's asleep. The excitement must have tired him out. His little face is so peaceful. Poor thing doesn't have a clue how much trouble he's in. How desperate his future is. How much he's in the poo, and not just in his bundle.

It's not fair. It's not his fault his parents were foreign. It's not his fault murdering thugs think Poland would be a nicer place if he was dead.

I think of what Gogol would have done if I hadn't taken him.

Shot him. Or stabbed him. Or smashed him against a wall.

No.

That's not going to happen.

I won't let it.

It won't be easy, and Gabriek won't like it, but I know this is what Mum and Dad and Zelda and Genia would have done.

'Don't worry,' I whisper to the sleeping little bundle. 'I'll look after you. You're my baby now.'

She's where I hope she'll be.

I spot her pink coat across food-drop square, which is starting to empty now the trucks have gone.

I hurry towards the girl.

She's with an elderly man. He's showing her something in his armpit. She peers at it. He buttons his shirt up and they talk.

What's going on?

The man hands the girl a bundle of something. Money, probably, because she counts it and puts it in her pocket.

She hands something to him. A small bottle, I think. If it's petrol, it's barely a squirt. And what does petrol have to do with armpits? I'm pretty sure it's no good for repelling fleas.

The elderly man scurries away. He doesn't look well. I hope whatever he's paid for gives him some medical relief for his armpit.

The girl glances around again and sees me.

I decide not to get bogged down asking her if she's had the experience to be treating armpits. And charging for it. I'm here for something more important.

'I've changed my mind,' I say to her. 'I'll join your gang.'

The girl looks at the baby.

'Not in America yet?' she says.

'His parents are dead,' I say. 'He's only got me. There are things I need. Powdered milk and nappies and disinfectant and real soap and real orange juice and real toilet paper.'

The girl frowns.

'No solid gold nappy pins?' she says.

I sigh. Sarcasm is the lowest form of wit, it's a medical fact.

'Do you want me or not?' I say. 'Medical and break-in services in return for baby supplies.'

The girl thinks about it.

She looks at the baby again.

'I've got a babysitter in my family,' I say. 'So I'll be available all hours.'

Actually I haven't got a clue how I'm going to persuade Gabriek to be a babysitter. I haven't even got a clue how I'm going to persuade him to let the baby live with us.

The girl grins.

'Alright,' she says.

I've just volunteered for a life of crime, so I don't have anything to grin about. But I find myself grinning back. It's another one of those awkward things that happens when you're thirteen. I don't stop, and the girl doesn't either.

Which is how come neither of us is keeping an eye out for danger.

Big hands grab me from behind.

I struggle in the powerful grip, desperately trying not to drop the baby. Images flash through my head of Gogol doing terrible things to us.

The girl looks like she's in shock.

She must know Gogol's reputation.

Then I realise these aren't Gogol's hands. They're too big and hairy. And the voice hissing in my ear about cheats and locks isn't Gogol's either.

'Mr Dimmi, sir,' I say. 'It's OK. It's fixed.'

I try to twist round to show him the lock in my bag. Which is very hard to do when both your hands are clutching a baby.

Suddenly Dimmi relaxes his grip.

I stumble and almost fall backwards. For a moment I concentrate on not dropping the baby, so at first I don't see what's happening.

Then I do.

Dimmi is standing there trembling, his eyes open wide.

And his mouth, because the girl has her gun jammed into it.

'Don't hurt him,' I say to her. 'He's a customer.'

It's good of her to help, but if that gun goes off it'll be a disaster for everyone. For Dimmi and his father and for Gabriek's business reputation. And criminal people like this girl can be unpredictable with guns, I've seen it happen.

Gently I pull her away from Dimmi.

The gun slides out of his mouth, wet with saliva.

Before Dimmi can get violent again, I reach under my coat and take the lock out of my medical bag and put it into his hands.

'There,' I say. 'All fixed. Sorry about the delay.'

Dimmi stares at it for a moment.

Then glares at me.

'We're never doing business with you ever again,' he says, and stamps away, giving a last nervous glance at the girl.

I look anxiously at the baby. Seeing all this violence isn't good for a young person. But the baby is sucking his tongue and chuckling at the girl. Clever little thing must know it's because of her I'll be able to keep his tummy full.

'Thanks,' I say to the girl.

She isn't looking at me or the baby. She's looking at Dimmi as he strides away across the square.

'Interesting,' she says. 'Anyone who cares that much about a door-lock must have some serious valuables to protect.'

'No,' I say. 'We can't. He's a customer.'

Never steal from a customer. It's Gabrick's other strictest rule.

I can tell from the girl's face she doesn't agree.

'You've got a lot to learn,' she says. 'Lesson one, toilet paper doesn't grow on trees.'

She looks across at Dimmi again.

For a second I think she's going to follow him.

But she doesn't. Because a truck roars out of nowhere and nearly runs us over, and while we're off-balance, we're grabbed.

This time it is Gogol's men.

Soon, I hope, the baby will stop crying.

'There, there, little bundle,' I whisper to him. 'It's OK.'

He doesn't stop crying. Because it's not OK. We're in a truck bouncing along streets very fast towards a scary thug called Gogol.

At least his men aren't using sacks this time.

Just guns to our heads.

And at least they're letting me hold the baby. His crying was getting on their nerves and they must have been told to deliver him alive.

I stroke the baby's head to comfort him.

'It's OK,' I say to him again, because you have to with babies. Plus there's a tiny chance it might turn out OK if I can think what to do.

As the baby whimpers and the truck speeds on, I glance at the girl. Her face is grim. I can't tell what she's thinking.

I silently plead with her to be sensible about her

gun, which the thug who shot the German boy took from her.

It's stuck in his belt.

She keeps looking at it.

Think, I say to her with my eyes. Even if you could grab it before he stops you, there are six of them and two of us. Be reasonable. There's a chance we can talk our way out of this.

I stroke the baby's head some more.

I'm trying to comfort all of us.

But I'm not doing a very good job because I can't stop thinking about the person we're being taken to. And what he'll do to us if I can't persuade him to be reasonable.

Gogol is in a school playground.

It's a cold day, but he's naked from the waist up, lying on his back lifting weights. Around him are other items of exercise equipment from the wrecked school gymnasium.

The school fence is still standing, so the truck parks outside. The men take me and the baby and the girl over to Gogol.

Gogol puts the weights down and stands up.

He's quite skinny, but the weights aren't.

'What's your name?' he says to me.

'Felix,' I say.

I don't say my family name. When a war's been on, people don't use family names much, there's no point.

'And yours?' Gogol says to the girl.

'Anya,' she says.

'Polish?' he says.

'Yes,' she says.

Gogol gives her a hard look, then nods.

I can see Anya wants to know what's going on. Why she's here.

Gogol looks at the baby and frowns.

I hold the bundle tighter.

'Please,' I say to Gogol. 'I'm sorry. I shouldn't have taken him. I'll make it up to you. If you let him live, I'll work for you for as long as you like.'

Gogol doesn't look at me.

He picks up a towel and wipes the sweat off his arms.

'This doesn't please me,' he says, 'what I have to do. But word gets around. And people must know what happens if they try to stop us doing our work.'

I know what Gogol's planning to do. I've known it since his men grabbed us in the square.

'It's just me,' I say to Gogol. 'I'm the only one you have to make an example of. Anya wasn't involved. She didn't try to stop you doing your work. It was just me.'

I put the baby into Anya's arms.

'Please,' I say to Gogol. 'Let them go. Just do it to me.'

Gogol takes the bundle from Anya and thrusts it back at me. Then he looks at Anya again as if he's only just recognising her.

'Petrol?' he says.

Anya nods.

Gogol looks at his men. A couple of them nod too.

With a weary sigh, Gogol waves Anya away.

Her head flops forward with relief as she realises she can go. I try to give her the baby again. Gogol slaps me. I manage to hang on to the bundle, but I have to sit down on a pile of mats.

Gogol grabs Anya's arm.

'Tell them,' he says to her. 'When they see the boy and the brat nailed to trees, tell them this is what will happen to them all if they interfere with our work.'

Anya nods.

She looks at me. I give her a pleading look back.

Please, take the baby.

'I'm sorry,' she says, then hugs her coat tightly round her and hurries away across the playground.

I stand up.

I'm young, I'm fit, my legs have never felt stronger. I could run, even with a baby . . .

Gogol shakes his head.

'Don't make me shoot you here,' he says. 'I want you where people can see you. One thing I learned from killing Nazis, bodies are easier to transport when they can still walk. But if I have to kill you here, I will.'

I can see he means it.

I sit back down.

Gogol lies back down and starts lifting again.

The other men take off their jackets and do some training themselves. Weights, punching bags, chin-ups on bars. None of them is more than half a metre away from a gun.

I glance over at their truck, still parked by the school fence.

It would be a fifty-metre dash, and if me and the baby were still alive when we got there, and if I could work out how to drive it . . .

Hang on, what's that under the truck?

I stare harder and my mouth falls open. A rubber tube is snaking out of the truck's petrol tank and disappearing underneath.

Something's moving under there.

Something pink.

I can't believe it.

She's stealing their petrol.

An innocent baby is lying here with a death sentence, and for her it's business as usual.

I try not to let despair get to me. But sometimes you can't help it. When armed men casually shoot innocent strangers, for example. Or when normal people pretend not to notice as their neighbours are hunted down. Or when you see petrol being more important than babies.

I just want to give up when I see that.

It makes me wish the war had destroyed everything so the world can start again. So maybe in a billion years there'll be some humans who'll know how to be loving and generous and—

An explosion rocks the playground.

Roaring sheets of fire fling Gogol's truck into the air, splitting it and twisting it and crashing it down, spewing flame and smoke.

I'm on my back on the ground, ears hurting, still clutching the baby.

What's going on? Are we under attack? Where's Anya?

Gogol and his men are on their feet, yelling.

Gunfire erupts all around us.

The men dive flat. I try to put my body over the baby without smothering him. Bullets are hissing everywhere.

I try to see who's shooting, but I can't.

A thought hits me.

Maybe nobody is shooting.

What if that was petrol exploding? And there was ammunition in the truck? Is the heat from an explosion enough to make ammunition fire itself?

I don't know for sure, but I'll take the risk.

I don't wait to ask the men where they store their bullets. I don't wait to see if Anya's OK.

This is our one chance.

I grab the baby and run.

Soon, I hope, we can get out of this sewer.

But not just yet.

Patience, little bundle. I know this is a very slow way home. I know we've been down here for hours. But a wise Jewish man said to me once, when you've got murdering brutes breathing down your neck, take your time.

I think it's worked. I haven't heard Gogol's men yelling for ages. I think they've gone to get another truck. To find more Ukrainians to kill. And wait for the day they can catch me on the street.

We're not worrying about that now.

We're looking on the bright side. Isn't it good how most of this city's plumbing has been broken for years so there's not much liquid down here? A bit of slime, yes, but that's better than poo water up to your pelvis.

Which you'd know about, little bundle.

And see this daylight ahead? By my calculations,

this is a bomb crater about two blocks from our place. We can climb out of the tunnel here and we'll almost be home.

Well done, little bundle. If you'd stopped sucking the sugar water and started crying, we'd probably be dead by now.

I tuck him inside my coat, ready for the climb.

Luckily this bomb crater is in the middle of a pickle factory. The pickles are long gone and so are the workers, so nobody will see us.

Except what's that?

Noises above us.

Oh no. It sounds like somebody creeping over the smashed tiles in the factory.

And I don't think it's just anybody.

Gogol's tricked me.

What was I thinking?

I should have known that a man who's killed as many people as he has wouldn't ever give up.

Footsteps coming closer.

He'll be sliding down the crater slope any second, planning to add us to his total.

No point trying to run. You can't run along a sewer. Not with a baby and slime.

I grab a broken chunk of brick. I'm not a fighter, but I'm all this baby's got. And I won't let him die without a fight.

Dust and small bits of rubble clatter down the slope. Should I hide the baby under this concrete ledge in case I lose the fight?

What would Gabriek do?

Apart from have a drink.

'It's OK,' I whisper to the baby as I put him under the ledge. 'I won't leave you.'

'Felix?'

That doesn't sound like Gogol. But it's hard to tell with the echo down here.

'Felix.'

I go weak with relief. I pick the baby up so he can see it's OK.

'Anya,' I say. 'Down here.'

She clambers down the slope. There's not much light so I can't see if she was hurt in the explosion. Her coat seems to be all in one piece and the rubber petrol hose looped over her shoulders seems to be too.

'Are you alright?' I say.

Anya nods, which is also a relief.

But there's a question I have to ask her.

'The truck,' I say. 'Was that an accident?'

She looks at me, her eyes bright in the gloom.

'What do you think?' she says.

I look at her for a moment.

'Thank you,' I say.

Anya gives a little shrug. She's staring at the chunk of brick in my hand.

'How did you know we'd be here?' I say.

'Easy,' says Anya. 'If I had a deranged killer after my guts, I'd come home by sewer too.'

She takes the chunk of brick from me.

'We think alike,' she says. 'You and me.'

That might be true, but it doesn't explain how she knows I live in this exact part of the city.

Anya tosses the chunk of brick away.

'Gogol will be after you too now,' I say.

'He didn't see me,' says Anya. 'I could have been a Ukrainian. Or a Jew. Fighting back.'

I nod. She could have been.

But will Gogol think so?

'You're the one,' says Anya. 'He'll really be after you now.'

'I'll lie low,' I say. 'Me and the baby. It's very secure where I live. You should lie low too, wherever you live.'

Anya gives me a look. I don't think she likes people telling her what to do.

'Where will you get all that stuff you need?' she says. 'The powdered milk and the orange juice and the diamond-studded toilet paper.'

It sounds crazy now, that list. What was I thinking?

'Just powdered milk,' I say. 'So far he's been living on bread soup and sugar water.'

'I know people who'd kill for a meal like that,' says Anya.

'He's a baby,' I say. 'He needs milk.'

He and I both need it. I need it to show I can look after a baby. So when I ask if the baby can live with us, there's a chance Gabriek will say yes rather than have a seizure.

Anya is silent for a moment.

'Felix,' she says. 'There's milk at my place. But if I take you there, do you swear to keep everything about the place a secret?'

I'm stunned, but I manage to nod.

'I know about security,' I say.

'Come on,' says Anya. 'We'll go through the alleys. Almost as safe and twice as quick.'

I can't help smiling.

We do think alike.

I follow her out of the tunnel, baby in my arms, careful not to lose my balance climbing up the crater.

This is incredibly generous of her.

Yes, I'm in her gang, but powdered milk is like gold. And these days you don't invite anyone home, not even so they can get bits of their bath out of your kitchen.

At last, I've met somebody in this tragic wreck of a city who still wants to be generous and get involved and take a risk.

It's our lucky day, little bundle.

Soon, I hope, we'll be at Anya's place.

When we get there, I'm going to give this hungry little bundle the biggest drink of milk a baby's ever had.

'Almost there,' says Anya.

I stare.

'Is that where you live?' I say.

She nods.

It's the only house still standing in this whole section of the street. One of the most amazing houses I've ever seen. And I've lived in a bunker in the forest with tree roots for walls and in a nunnery in the mountains with real nuns.

This house is huge. If all the other houses around here used to be like this one, people must have needed telephones just to speak to their neighbours.

As we get closer to Anya's place, I see that the windows are boarded up, but apart from that there's hardly any shell or bomb damage. Just a few cracks and scorch marks on the walls and a bit of guttering flapping loose.

On the front gate is a large sign.

Lipzyk Orphanage.

It all makes sense. We've been talking about our parents and Anya's were killed by the Nazis too. And orphanages probably get special supplies of powdered milk.

I realise how lucky Anya is. There are hardly any orphanages, and millions of kids with dead parents. So the orphans are usually kicked out before they get to Anya's age.

I congratulate her.

'What's your secret?' I say.

She gives me a strange look. Doesn't reply.

I let it go. Because I see something at the side of the house. A wooden cart with two big wheels and two shafts for a horse to pull it. No chain or padlock or anything. I'm amazed nobody's stolen it.

Then I see why.

A sheet hanging from a big tree stump in the front garden.

A big red X painted on it.

Typhus.

I stop and glance at Anya, who suddenly doesn't seem so lucky after all.

If you've got a disease like typhus at home, you're probably going to live about a week. So are the people in your family. Babies last about a day.

I hold my baby tighter.

Anya doesn't have a rash, or a fever, or any signs of chronic brain swelling. Which I'm glad about for her sake as well as ours.

Anya sees me looking.

'That isn't real,' she says quietly. 'It's just for security.'

I'm relieved. Normally I don't approve of lying about illness, but these are difficult times.

Anya ties a large handkerchief over her nose and mouth. I get what she's doing. She hands one to me. I do the same, then pull the edge of the baby's bundle up over his mouth so that if people are watching, it looks like we're protecting him from germs too.

This is excellent security. I'm impressed.

Gabriek would be as well.

I'm about to ask Anya whose idea it was, but she opens the front gate and puts her hand on my arm.

'Tread only where I tread,' she says.

I look at her, puzzled. She leans closer to me.

'Mines,' she says.

My tummy goes tight with shock.

'Mines?' I squeak.

'Security,' she says.

I'm stunned. On the way here she wouldn't tell me about her place. Just kept saying, you'll see.

Anya is already heading up the front path.

I follow, treading only where she treads. She steps over two bits of paving stone, then walks on three, then misses one, then I lose count and just concentrate on putting my feet exactly where she puts hers.

The baby whimpers in my arms.

Poor little thing doesn't have a clue how much danger we're in. If there wasn't powdered milk at the other end, and if I didn't need it so much for a hungry bundle and a grumpy Gabriek, I wouldn't be doing this.

We arrive at the front door. I take a few deep relieved breaths through the hanky.

'Where did the mines come from?' I say.

Now the war's over, new mines must be hard to get. And second-hand ones can be very unstable. Hail storms can set them off, I've seen it happen.

'Good question,' says Anya. 'The mines. Let me see.'

She frowns, thinking.

'From my imagination,' she says.

I stare at her.

'Sorry,' she says. 'When I saw how impressed you are by security, I couldn't resist.'

Her eyes show she's grinning under her hanky.

It's not funny. I've seen what mines can do to people, including babies. I'm about to tell her that, but before I can, her eyes stop sparkling.

'Also,' she says, 'it was a little test. To see if you can do what you're told.'

I swallow uncomfortably.

What does she mean?

You know how when you meet someone who's scary and then she saves your life and is so friendly and generous you feel like you're getting to know her and you discover she thinks like you but then she starts behaving strangely and you realise you barely know her at all?

I hope that doesn't happen with every girl I meet, because it's really confusing.

I try to think of something else to say. Even though I'm confused, I want her to see I'm still grateful.

Anya takes a key from her coat pocket and puts it into the lock on the front door. A very beautiful lock. Double-action lever, hardened steel, rare bitted key. Impossible to crack.

'Great lock,' I say. 'Gabriek would love to see that.'

Anya looks at me.

'He can't,' she says. 'I'm only allowed to bring kids here.'

I frown.

More security, I suppose.

Sort of makes sense in an orphanage.

I want to remind Anya I'm not a child. But I don't in case she changes her mind and a desperate bundle stays hungry.

Soon, I hope, we can get out of here.

I know it's a bit early to be saying that as we follow Anya into the house. I haven't met the orphanage adults yet or introduced them to this little bundle or thanked them for the powdered milk.

Or been given it.

But I've just had a horrible thought. Gabriek was expecting me back from the military welfare office ages ago. He asked me to come straight home to tell him where the baby was going.

He'll be worried. When Gabriek gets worried, he starts drinking. People with a lot of alcohol inside them don't like unpleasant surprises, it's a medical fact. So me coming back home with an unwelcome baby could be a disaster.

I try to think of happier things. Like powdered milk. I hope the baby's thinking about happier things too. He looks like he is. He's gazing up at a beautiful chandelier above us in the entrance hall.

I gaze too. It's the biggest chandelier I've ever seen. A hundred candles at least. Before the war, when it was undamaged, it probably had two hundred.

Amazing.

A boy a bit younger than me is standing at the top of a step-ladder, polishing the crystal candle-holders one by one.

Poor kid. He's going to be there for hours.

The boy is concentrating so hard on not spilling any wax and not falling off the ladder, he doesn't notice us at first.

'Hello, Bolek,' says Anya. 'This is Felix.'

Bolek glances down.

'Hello,' he says.

'Hello,' I say, wondering where I've seen him before. He looks sort of familiar.

But I don't wonder about that for long, because suddenly I smell it. The musty woody leathery smell I've missed so much. The wonderful warm sweet dusty smell that only comes from one thing.

Books.

I breathe it in. You just don't get this smell with a library of two medical textbooks.

The last time I smelled this I was six.

In our bookshop.

With Mum and Dad.

I can't stop myself. I want to get closer to the books. See them. Touch them. Stick my nose right into them.

I head up the hallway, not caring that visitors

should let hosts lead the way in case any of the floorboards have got dry rot or bomb damage.

I step into a large room.

Walls of books, floor to ceiling. Almost none of the shelves are broken. And there are ladders so you can get to the top shelves.

Just like we had.

My eyes are going a bit emotional. I only realise there's someone else in the room when I see a blurry movement.

Suddenly I feel very rude. Wandering into somebody's book room without being invited.

'Sorry,' I say, rubbing my eyes.

'No need,' says a deep soft voice.

I blink.

A man is looking at me with an amused smile. He's tall with neatly combed hair. He's wearing a very clean suit without a single crease showing. The boy in the hallway must be good at washing and ironing too.

'And who are you?' says the man.

His smile is warm and friendly, which you don't often see these days.

'I'm Felix,' I say.

'Welcome, Felix,' he says. 'I'm Doctor Lipzyk.'

He holds out his hand.

I shake it.

Anya comes in. She's taken off her coat. She points at mine and I take it off while she holds the baby.

I feel a bit out of place in this big luxury room with its own chandelier and fireplace and a rug with hardly any holes and millions of books. If the curtains in here are made from sacks, they're very high quality ones.

'This is the person I was telling you about,' Anya says to Doctor Lipzyk. 'He's going to be a doctor.'

Doctor Lipzyk smiles.

'Always a pleasure to meet a colleague,' he says.

I don't feel embarrassed because Doctor Lipzyk sounds like he means it.

Anya hands the baby back to me.

'Patient of yours?' says Doctor Lipzyk.

'Sort of,' I say.

'May I?' he says.

Doctor Lipzyk takes the baby and examines him, feeling his arms and legs and tummy and looking closely into his eyes and ears and mouth.

'Few flea bites,' murmurs Doctor Lipzyk, 'but otherwise seems quite healthy.'

'Felix has adopted him,' says Anya. 'I said you might be able to give him some milk.'

Doctor Lipzyk doesn't scowl like most people would if you asked them to give away food. He just nods and says, 'Fresh or powdered?'

I stare at him.

At first I think he's joking. In this city, fresh milk is rarer than full sets of parents.

'Powdered would be best,' says Anya. 'So he can get it home without spilling it or getting killed for it.'

Doctor Lipzyk nods and hands the baby back to me.

'Let me organise that,' he says. 'And I'll mix up some tonic drops. Your little one's looking a bit anaemic.'

'Thank you,' I say.

Doctor Lipzyk is amazing. He's exactly the sort of doctor I want to be. Kind, skilful and excellent at making people feel relaxed and like they've got good vocabularies.

'Excuse me for saying this, Felix,' says Doctor Lipzyk gently. 'But that baby needs a bath.'

'I know,' I say hastily. 'I'm planning to give him one.'

Doctor Lipzyk smiles.

'Look after our visitors, Anya,' he says, and goes.

I turn to Anya.

'You're so lucky,' I say. 'Living here.'

I know this is the second time I've said it, but I can't help myself. She is lucky.

Anya frowns. And shrugs.

I'm amazed. How could anybody not be grateful about living here?

I look around at the bookshelves again. And notice something even more amazing.

It's so amazing I don't believe it at first.

I look more closely, shelf after shelf.

They're all medical books.

'Anya,' I say weakly. 'Would you mind holding the baby again?'

She takes him from me. I take a book from a shelf. A book about bones in humans, including, I'm interested to see, leg bones.

'Felix,' says a voice.

At first I don't know where I am. I'm studying a colour illustration of a spleen and I don't want to take my eyes off it.

'Felix.'

I look up.

Anya is standing there, holding the baby.

I blink. The baby is about two shades pinker than I've ever seen him. And his bundle is different. It's clean and new and fresh.

'Thanks,' I say.

Doctor Lipzyk is standing behind her, smiling. He hands me a paper bag and a small bottle. The bag has powdered milk in it, and the bottle has tonic drops.

'Thank you very much, sir,' I say.

'Give him two drops three times a day in boiled water,' says Doctor Lipzyk. 'First ones as soon as you get home.'

My tummy lurches.

Home.

Gabriek.

I haven't got a clue how long I've been here.

'Before you go,' says Doctor Lipzyk, 'sit down and have some hot chocolate. And some warm milk for the baby.'

A boy and a girl are standing next to him, both about my age. Both are carrying trays.

I can't say no. They've already made it. Plus I haven't had chocolate for years.

I'll drink it quickly.

We all sit at a table. Doctor Lipzyk pours from a silver jug and hands me a cup. I gulp the hot drink. It's the most delicious thing I've ever tasted.

But even hot chocolate isn't enough to stop me feeling anxious about Gabriek.

I'll give the baby the warm milk and we'll go.

It takes me ages to drip the milk out of the bottle into the baby's mouth. And mop up the rest with the towel an older girl kindly brings.

Now I'm frantic at how late we are.

I stand up.

'Sorry to be rude, sir,' I say to Doctor Lipzyk. 'But we have to go. Thank you for everything. You're very kind and your orphanage is brilliant.'

'Very nice of you to say so,' says Doctor Lipzyk. 'I do what I can. This is a dark and difficult time for young people. Many go astray.'

I'm not sure exactly what he means, so it's hard to reply.

Then it gets even harder because the boy who brought the hot chocolate clears away the cups, and suddenly I realise something.

Him and the other boy in the hall cleaning the chandelier, I've seen them both before. On the back of an army food truck.

They're both in Anya's gang.

Which is extremely confusing.

Why would people living in the most luxurious orphanage in Europe secretly run around the city in grubby coats stealing petrol?

I manage to finish thanking Doctor Lipzyk, and Anya sees me to the door.

In the hallway she holds the baby while I stow the powdered milk and tonic drops safely in the secret coat pockets Gabriek made. I do it with my back to her so they stay secret.

While I'm doing that, I ask Anya what's going on. If I'm going to be in her gang, I need to know what's what.

There's no reply.

I turn to her.

She's not there. The baby is lying on the carpet and the front door is open. I see Anya in the garden, kneeling in front of a couple of spindly rose bushes.

I pick the baby up and go out. At first I think Anya is smelling the roses, then I see she's not.

She's being sick into them.

'Are you alright?' I say.

Anya finishes throwing up, wipes her mouth, grabs a spade, and covers the sick with dirt.

She turns to me, her face hard and angry.

'You shouldn't have seen that,' she says. 'And if you ever tell Doctor Lipzyk or anyone else, I'll make you wish you hadn't.'

She goes inside and shuts the door.

I stare at the spade and the patch of dirt.

Now I'm even more confused. If you live with the world's kindest doctor and you're not well, why wouldn't you want him to know?

Soon, I hope, this bag of powdered milk and this bottle of tonic drops will make everything OK with Gabriek. And he'll say yes, of course the baby can live with us.

I hope.

Gabriek opens the door after I do our knock and I go in.

'Sorry I'm late,' I say. 'A few things happened.'

Gabriek doesn't ask what. Just looks at the baby. Then steps past me and closes the door.

My heart valves are hurting. And not just from the stress of rushing back here and keeping my eyes alert for Gogol.

'So,' says Gabriek, looking at the baby again. 'Welfare wouldn't take him?'

'I tried,' I say. 'I peed on a guard's foot and everything.'

Gabriek sits on the stool next to our little stove. I see he's been cooking a turnip on the hot pipes he invented to stop the smoke escaping.

That's not why he's sitting down. His vodka mug is next to the stool. He picks it up and swallows a mouthful.

My heart sinks. But I'm prepared for this.

I have a secret weapon.

'Look,' I say, pulling out the bag of milk powder.

It doesn't seem as big as it did at the orphanage. Maybe chandeliers make things look bigger.

Doesn't matter.

'It's genuine milk,' I say. 'And look, tonic drops. I know where to get more. So the baby will always be fed and healthy.'

'Good,' says Gabriek. 'Whoever ends up looking after him will be glad of that. I had a word to a few customers today, just in case. I'll speak to more tomorrow.'

I have to sit down too. Not because of vodka, because of frustration. I plonk onto the other stool, hugging the baby to me.

Gabriek has a good heart, but he also has the most stubborn brain ever to occupy a cranial cavity.

'This baby needs us,' I say. 'Your mechanical skill and my medical skill. We're the perfect parents.'

Gabriek takes another swig from his mug.

I'm not convincing him.

The baby starts to cry. Not loudly, but enough to remind Gabriek that I'm holding a security risk to my chest.

I try another secret weapon.

Gabriek's good heart.

I put the sobbing baby on the floor and wash my hands in the basin. When I turn back, the baby is still on the floor, still sobbing.

Gabriek hasn't picked him up.

I sit back down, get out the sugar water and let the baby suck my finger.

'You and me,' I say to Gabriek, 'we've only got each other. So if anything happened to either of us, the other one would be on his own. But not if we had this baby with us. If I got killed, you'd –'

'Don't,' says Gabriek.

He takes another swig.

I feel tears of frustration pricking my eyes and I don't want them to. I unwrap the baby and hold him out, pink and soft and naked and defenceless.

'They called him an ape,' I say.

Gabriek's eyes narrow.

'What?' he says.

'An ape,' I say.

'Who?'

I stop myself. I still haven't told Gabriek about Gogol, and now is a bad time. If Gabriek knows I'm on a death list because of this baby, there's no way the little bundle will be allowed to stay here.

'People I did some medical work for,' I say. 'Who didn't like him. Or his parents.'

'Little fella must be Ukrainian,' mutters Gabriek. 'Ape is a word the ignorant and the vile use for Ukrainians.'

Gabriek doesn't say anything else. Just stares at the baby. But I can see he's more upset than he wants to show.

Sleep.

Please go to sleep.

It'll be dawn soon. You've drunk so much milk I've lost count. We've run out of nappies. My spare clothes are all sodden. My bed has absorbed so much of your pee it's sagging at the sides.

Please.

The baby obviously doesn't understand the words please, sleep or sagging.

He just carries on gurgling in my arms.

I'm exhausted. But not just from lack of sleep. From all the thinking. About what I'll do if Gabriek refuses to let the baby stay.

I've decided the next safest thing would be for the baby to live with his own people. Ukrainian people. So, if he can't stay here, I'd have to find some of them.

But I don't want to think about that now.

I put the baby back down on my bed, lie down next to him and try to think about something I can control rather than something I can't.

A plan I've thought up to get Gogol off our backs. To make him totally lose interest in killing me and the baby.

By making him think we're both already dead.

Simple, but I think it'll work.

All I need are a couple of bodies. Which are easy to come by these days. People die of hunger all the time in this city and nobody cares. If I can't find the bodies of a baby and a thirteen-year-old in a couple of days, I'm just not trying. Then all I've got to do is put some bullet holes in them and get them delivered to Gogol by somebody believable.

Dimmi maybe.

Or somebody in Anya's gang.

Or . . .

The baby is gazing up at me, eyes wide and fixed on my face.

I can see what he's thinking.

You're a doctor. Doctors don't do horrible things like that with innocent people's bodies. Get a grip.

He's right.

But these are desperate times, little bundle. Most people in the world seem to be doing things that would have horrified them in the old days. And made their parents very upset.

Perhaps I have to as well.

I can't decide now. I need to sleep. My eyes are sagging even more than my mattress.

Please.

I half open my eyes.

Light is seeping through the cracks between the curtains. Not dull dawn light, bright daylight.

I've slept in.

I open my eyes wide and panic jolts through me.

The baby's not here.

I'm alone in the bed.

I sit up and peer frantically around. If Gabriek's gone too . . . if he's taken the baby . . .

He hasn't. He's asleep in his bed, lying on his back, snoring softly, the baby asleep on his chest.

I flop back down, weak with relief.

And knock the tap I got for Gabriek onto the floor. It clatters across the wooden boards.

Gabriek opens his eyes.

'A baby needs a name,' he says. 'We can't just call him little bundle.'

I stare at Gabriek, taking this in.

'Only one Ukrainian name I can think of,' says Gabriek. 'Pavlo. It belonged to a partisan who took a bullet protecting my back. Will that do?'

'Yes,' I say. 'Yes, it will.'

'And we'll need milk,' says Gabriek. 'A regular supply. Paid for, so we can depend on it.'

'Yes,' I say, my heart valves doing cartwheels. 'I agree.'

What I really want to say is thank you, thank you, thank you, and fling my arms round them both. But I don't want to overdo it. Gabriek isn't really a morning person.

'The doctor you told me about last night,' says Gabriek. 'Give me his address and I'll go and see him and arrange something.'

I hesitate.

'The person who took me there,' I say, 'she made

me promise I won't tell anybody where they are.'

Gabriek frowns.

'I'll go,' I say.

Gabriek thinks about this. He understands about promises and security. I think he also understands this is something I should do because I was the one who brought Pavlo into our family.

'Alright,' says Gabriek. 'But if he won't deal with you straight, tell him to meet me in food-drop square.'

'I will,' I say.

I pause a moment, struggling with my thoughts. I know I should tell Gabriek about Gogol. Me and Gabriek never keep anything from each other. You can't survive for two years in a hole if you and the person looking after you can't trust each other.

But knowing about Gogol will just make Gabriek stressed and anxious. And when that happens, so does cabbage vodka.

I'm thirteen now. It's time I took responsibility for solving some of our problems myself.

Starting with Gogol.

'Are you alright?' says Gabriek, looking at me, concerned.

'Lots to do,' I say. 'Just preparing myself.'

Gabriek nods. He's done a lot of difficult things in his life. Including killing Nazis, and killing is the thing he hates most in the whole world.

I look at his kind weather-beaten face and I feel my cardiovascular system glowing with love.

It's amazing. Gabriek has given me so much, and yet he's still got enough generosity left over to give shelter to a baby he hardly knows.

'Are you sure you're alright?' says Gabriek.

'Totally,' I say.

Which is true.

So far.

Soon, I hope, that man's face will heal.

It must be very badly injured to be completely wrapped in bandages like that. I'm amazed he can see through such tiny eyeholes.

He must be able to, because as we pass each other in Doctor Lipzyk's front garden he doesn't bump into me or trip over a paving stone.

Just hurries away.

Poor man. But at least he's got a really good doctor. If anybody can cure a face that's suffering from shrapnel or other bomb damage, Doctor Lipzyk can.

I knock on the front door of the orphanage.

After a few moments, Doctor Lipzyk opens it. He's reading a piece of paper and doesn't look up.

'If you've forgotten something,' he says crossly, 'make it quick. Those bandages need to be out of sight.'

I pull the hanky off my face so Doctor Lipzyk

can see it's me. He looks up with a cross expression, then blinks, startled.

I'm a bit startled too. Doctor Lipzyk is wearing a white medical gown with quite a few smears of blood on it.

'Forgive me, Felix,' says Doctor Lipzyk. 'I assumed you were someone else. Come in.'

I go in.

'I hope this isn't a bad time,' I say.

Doctor Lipzyk can probably remember when all his neighbours had telephones as well as houses and people rang first before they dropped in.

'Not at all, Felix,' says Doctor Lipzyk. 'Though unfortunately Anya isn't here.'

'That's OK,' I say. 'I've come to see you.'

'Always a pleasure,' says Doctor Lipzyk. 'In fact I've been expecting you.'

I think I know why.

I explain to him how grateful me and Gabriek are for the powdered milk and how we wouldn't dream of accepting any more without paying for it. And how we hope he's OK about that because we'll need quite a lot.

'Which we'll definitely pay for,' I say. 'Sometimes with actual money, but also with things you need. We can get really good parts for wardrobes and buckets and all kinds of security equipment. And if anything ever goes wrong here in the house, Gabriek can come and fix it.'

Doctor Lipzyk nods thoughtfully.

'Thank you, Felix,' he says. 'I'm sure we can come to an arrangement.'

He looks like he means it, which gives me the courage to move on.

'There is one other thing, sir,' I say.

'What's that?' says Doctor Lipzyk.

'I was wondering,' I say, 'if I could have another look at your library? I promise I'll be very careful.'

Doctor Lipzyk smiles.

'Of course you can, Felix,' he says. 'Here, let me take your coat.'

I slip my coat off and Doctor Lipzyk hangs it up. Then leads me into the book room.

'I'm very fortunate to have such a fine medical library,' says Doctor Lipzyk. 'When the university was bombed, many rare volumes came into my possession. It seems only fair that I should share my good fortune. So, Felix, from now on I want you to regard this library as yours, to use whenever you like.'

I stare at him.

'Thank you,' I squeak.

It's hard to stay calm when your medical library has just increased from two books to about a thousand.

'Make yourself at home,' says Doctor Lipzyk. 'I'll get cleaned up and we'll talk some more.'

He goes out.

I accept Doctor Lipzyk's kind invitation.

I make myself completely at home. I walk along

the shelves, studying the titles. I know exactly what I'm looking for.

A book with all the medical reasons why people throw up.

'Quite the bookworm,' says Doctor Lipzyk.

I jump.

Look up guiltily.

Slide the book I was studying back onto the shelf.

Doctor Lipzyk has changed out of his medical gown. I haven't got a clue how much time has passed. I think it's still daytime, but with the windows boarded up it's hard to tell. I could look at my watch, but that would be rude when a person's just started a conversation.

'Is there any area of medicine that particularly interests you, Felix?' asks Doctor Lipzyk.

I can't say vomiting. That's confidential between me and Anya, even though she's not my patient exactly.

'Anatomy,' I say, which is also true. 'I want to know more about the human body.'

Doctor Lipzyk smiles in a way that shows he understands.

'A very important area of medicine,' he says.

He points to the shelves.

'Many fine works of anatomy here,' he continues. 'But, Felix, never forget you have with you at all times the finest work of anatomy ever created.'

I don't understand.

'Put your hands on your chest,' says Doctor Lipzyk. 'Palms down. Press firmly. Now slide them slowly towards your legs.'

I do it, pressing firmly. As I move my hands downwards, I can feel my body parts under my clothes.

'Pectoralis major,' says Doctor Lipzyk. 'Sternum, aorta, transverse abdominis, costal cartilage, rectus abdominis.'

I understand.

My body is a library too.

It's an exciting thought. But I still need books to learn what's what. I bet Doctor Lipzyk didn't learn all his knowledge just from feeling his anatomy.

'Keep going,' says Doctor Lipzyk.

I move my hands over my hips towards the top of my legs.

'Pelvis,' says Doctor Lipzyk. 'Sigmoid colon, iliotibial tract . . .'

He stops. I stop too.

'What happened to your legs?' he says after a moment.

I tell him about the two years I spent hiding from the Nazis in a hole under a barn.

He frowns as he hears about it. Most people do.

'It wasn't too bad,' I say. 'I did lots of thinking. And Gabriek taught me how to mend things.'

'Felix,' says Doctor Lipzyk, 'may I examine your legs? I have a particular interest in the effects of trauma on bone and tissue and I may be able to help you.'

'Yes,' I say. 'Thanks.'

Gabriek and I have talked about whether medical science could help my legs. I think it probably could, but it would take a lot of money and medicine, and that's unlikely in a world where people are dying of coughs.

'Could you please take off your trousers,' says Doctor Lipzyk, closing the door.

The idea feels a bit strange in somebody else's living room. Specially as I'm not wearing any underpants. They got left behind in the flea cellar and I haven't wanted to trouble Gabriek for new ones.

I explain this to Doctor Lipzyk.

He sighs.

'As a doctor, Felix,' he says, 'you'll learn that in medicine there's no place for feelings, including embarrassment. You'll come to see the body for what it is – just a very clever machine.'

I'm not sure I totally agree with this, but I take my trousers off anyway.

'Now,' says Doctor Lipzyk. 'Face me, please.'

I do.

Doctor Lipzyk stands in front of me and looks at the lower part of my body. For about one second. Then he scowls and turns away.

'Get dressed,' he says. 'I can't help you.'

I'm shocked. If a brilliant doctor like him can

tell in one second that he can't help me, my legs must be a disaster. Doctor Lipzyk has his back to me. He doesn't even want to look at them.

The door crashes open.

It's Anya.

She's got her coat on, so she must have just come home. She's out of breath and looks upset.

'Felix,' she says, 'I've got some bad news.'

She stops and stares at me.

My heart valves are in my throat. I'm naked and she's looking. I grab my clothes and hold them in front of my private part.

'Anya,' snaps Doctor Lipzyk. 'How dare you burst in here when I'm with a patient.'

Anya doesn't seem to know what to say next. She glares at Doctor Lipzyk, who is glaring at her.

'Leave us,' says Doctor Lipzyk.

He's talking to Anya, not me.

'No,' says Anya. 'There's something I have to tell Felix. It's important.'

'Come with me, Anya,' says Doctor Lipzyk, his voice quieter now but still furious. 'I've got something I need to say to you. I think you'll agree it's just as important.'

He grabs Anya by the shoulder and pushes her out of the room, closing the door behind them.

I'm so shaken by everything that's just happened I take twice as long to get my trousers back on.

What could Anya's bad news be?

Gabriek said he'd stay in the hideout with baby

Pavlo today, safe and secure, so it can't be anything that's happened to them.

There's a knock on the door.

Bolek the chandelier-cleaning gang boy comes in. 'Doctor Lipzyk said to give you this,' he says.

He hands me a cup of hot chocolate.

'Thanks,' I say.

That's good of Doctor Lipzyk, trying to cheer me up. He's a kind man. I don't blame him for being a bit grumpy just now. It's only natural when your mission is to heal and you come across legs that are hopeless.

I have a sad thought. I wonder if this kind man knows that some of the orphans he's caring for are in a gang?

Before I can ask Bolek, Doctor Lipzyk comes in with Anya.

Bolek leaves.

'Felix,' says Doctor Lipzyk, 'Anya wishes to apologise for her rudeness.'

'Sorry,' says Anya.

I can tell from her eyes that she's not.

'Now,' says Doctor Lipzyk to Anya. 'What is it you need to tell Felix?'

There's something in Doctor Lipzyk's voice that makes me feel a bit strange. Like he already knows what Anya needs to tell me.

'It's Gogol,' Anya says to me. 'He's put word out about you and the baby. He's offering a reward. A thousand zloty for you both. Dead.'

I take a sip of hot chocolate to make me feel better. It doesn't.

A thousand zloty is a lot of money. A person could buy a year's supply of eggs for a thousand zloty, and still have enough left over for a frying pan. In the future you'll probably be able to get a pair of dud legs fixed up for a thousand zloty.

This is serious.

I tell Doctor Lipzyk and Anya about my plan to fool Gogol into thinking that me and Pavlo are dead.

As I'm telling them about the bodies I'll need, I suddenly know I can't do it. Pavlo is right. I'm a doctor. And I can tell that Anya and Doctor Lipzyk don't think it's something I should do either.

I switch to my number two plan.

'I'll offer Gogol a deal,' I say. 'If he promises to leave the baby alone, I'll work for him for nothing. Medical services, weapon repairs, anything he wants. For the rest of my life.'

But even as I say this, I'm not sure if I can do that either. Repair his weapons so he can shoot more innocent people.

'Felix,' says Anya. 'There's another part to Gogol's reward. He's offering an extra thousand zloty for you and the baby alive.'

'Alive?' I say.

Anya nods.

I think about this. Then I try not to. If Gogol wants us dead but he's prepared to pay twice as much for us alive, the reason is too scary and horrible to think about.

'Trickery won't change his mind,' says Doctor Lipzyk. 'Neither will medical services and weapon repairs. He can get those anywhere. But you're on the right track, Felix. If you can find something this man wants, really wants, he'll do a deal. Everybody wants something.'

I look at them both helplessly.

What would a murdering patriot thug want more than gruesome revenge and showing the world he's still the boss?

'Anya and I have had a thought,' says Doctor Lipzyk. 'But I'm going to leave Anya to tell you about it because I have to see another patient. I think you're going to be alright, Felix. There's one little thing you can do for me, and then you're going to be fine.'

He reaches out to touch my shoulder, has second thoughts about it, and goes out.

I feel weak with relief. If Doctor Lipzyk thinks me and Pavlo are going to be OK, we probably will be.

I wait for Anya to explain their idea to me.

But all she does is go out into the hall and get my coat.

'I'll tell you on the way,' she says.

Soon, I hope, Anya will slow down a bit and start talking.

So far all we've done is walk very fast to a different part of the city. With Anya ignoring all my questions.

'Gastroenteritis?' I say, not giving up. 'Migraine? Duodenal ulcer? Battle fatigue? Cholera?'

When a person throws up and wants to keep it a secret, chances are it's happened more than once. Which means it could be something serious.

Anya just glares at me and keeps walking.

'None of your business,' she mutters.

She's as stubborn as Gabriek.

Plus I think she might be feeling shy because of the others. Bolek is with us and so are the other three gang boys who live at the orphanage. I think she's worried they'll hear, even though they dropped back a bit when I whispered to them that me and Anya need to have a private conversation. It's good to see that gang members can respect medical confidentiality.

'I'll tell you when I'm ready,' says Anya. 'If you ask me again, I'll shoot you.'

I sigh. Doctor Lipzyk is right. It's not easy for doctors when patients get embarrassed.

I change the subject.

'This idea of yours and Doctor Lipzyk's,' I say. 'What is it exactly I have to do?'

All I know so far is that it involves something Gogol wants. Something I hope will get good protection for me and Pavlo.

'Be patient,' says Anya. 'You'll find out soon.'

I sigh again. I know we have to keep our eyes open for Gogol and his men, plus anyone who likes the idea of a two-thousand-zloty reward. But it is possible to be alert to danger and talk at the same time. I've done it lots.

'Here we are,' says Anya.

The other boys catch up with us and we go down a side street.

Halfway along the street we clamber over piles of bricks into the living room of a downstairs apartment.

I stare, surprised.

Standing in the middle of the living-room floor is the wooden cart from the orphanage.

Anya must have organised this earlier today. She must have set up this mysterious plan to help me as soon as she heard that Gogol was after me.

I've never met anyone like her.

How can one person be so thoughtful and generous, and so confusing and frustrating?

'Into position,' says Anya. 'Heads down.'

We huddle down behind the bricks, watching an apartment building across the street. One with most of its apartments still there.

'They usually leave about now,' says Anya.

'Who?' I say.

I'm grateful, but also frustrated. Friends shouldn't keep each other in the dark, that's my motto.

Anya sees my face.

'Do you know what penicillin is?' she says.

I look at her. I may not be as experienced as Doctor Lipzyk, but I'm not a beginner.

I tell her about the tiny precious amount of penicillin we had when I was with the partisans in the forest. Precious because it was a wonder medicine that killed germs and cured people like nothing else. A tiny amount because it cost a fortune on the black market.

'Still does,' says Anya 'Makes powdered milk look cheap as brick-dust.'

'What about it?' I say.

'We're pretty sure,' says Anya, 'that if we offer Gogol enough penicillin, he'll agree to lay off you and the baby. He's lost men to gangrene lately, plus if he has any of it left over, he can sell it for a lot of money.'

'Where would we get it?' I say.

'That's not the problem,' says Anya. 'We've got plenty.'

I stare at her. Does she mean her and Doctor Lipzyk? They've got penicillin they'd give to Gogol? That seems amazingly generous, even for them.

'So what is the problem?' I say.

'Remember our conversation at the house?' says Anya. 'About how everybody wants something?'

I nod. Doctor Lipzyk said it.

'Well,' says Anya, 'over there is something Doctor Lipzyk wants.'

She points across to the apartment building.

'You should see it,' says one of the gang boys. 'It's amazing.'

'Vladek is our climber,' says Anya. 'He's been up onto their skylight.'

Vladek, who's about my age but small and skinny like a lot of good climbers, grins proudly.

'Nearly killed myself,' he says. 'Building's solid, but the tiles are ancient. Crumbly as army biscuits, you know, the really crumbly ones with the mould on them.'

'What is it Dr Lipzyk wants from over there?' I say to Anya impatiently.

'Paintings,' she says. 'Old paintings. There's an apartment up there full of them.'

'From museums,' says Vladek. 'Old masterpieces. Very rare and precious. I sketched some and Anya checked in books.'

'Vladek's a bit of an artist too,' says Anya.

I don't chat with Vladek about his art experience because I'm starting to understand what all this has got to do with me.

'It's a simple swap,' says Anya. 'The paintings go to Doctor Lipzyk's place, the penicillin goes to Gogol, you and the baby go around the city unharmed. With all the milk powder you want.'

'But only if I break into that apartment for you,' I say. 'Only if I get the lock open.'

Anya nods.

'Why are you bothering with the front door?' I say. 'There's a skylight. Take the paintings out through the skylight, onto the cart, off you go.'

'Skylight's too small,' says Anya.

'Roof's like biscuits,' says Vladek.

'There are people in some of the other apartments,' says Bolek. 'We can't make any noise.'

I think about this.

'What if I can't handle the lock?' I say. 'What if I can't open it?'

'You will,' says Anya.

She puts her finger to her lips and signals to us to duck lower behind the bricks. She points across the street.

'Owners of the paintings,' she whispers.

'Temporary owners,' murmurs Vladek.

I peer across the street.

Two men are coming out of the apartment building. One big and one small. I stare at them.

Dimmi and his father.

My brain races. Anya must have come here yesterday. To see what Dimmi's lock was protecting. And told Doctor Lipzyk about the paintings.

Is that why she took me to her house in the first place?

Has this been their plan all along?

I feel anger burning my rectus abdominis. This whole thing has just been Anya and Doctor Lipzyk taking advantage of a hungry baby to get their greedy hands on some valuable paintings.

'I'm not doing it,' I say. 'They're Gabriek's clients. If I rob them and people find out, Gabriek won't have a customer left in this city. I'm not doing that to him.'

Anya gives me a scornful look.

'They won't find out,' she says. 'Nobody will know.'

I give her a scornful look back. How can you trust the word of somebody who sets you up and uses you and lives in a big luxury house and can't even keep her coat clean?

'I'm not taking that chance,' I say. 'Forget it.'

I stand up and walk away.

I make sure it's in the opposite direction to Dimmi and his father, but I walk away.

Soon, I hope, I'll learn to be less emotional.

To think things through. To say, 'Could I please have a few hours to weigh all that up?' Which is what I should have said to Anya.

Because here I am, hurrying home along a dark street like I've done a million times before, and I've never felt so anxious.

Two thousand zloty.

That's what a ruthless killer will spend to get his hands on me and Pavlo. My only way to stop him is to maybe ruin the life of my dearest friend, who I owe my life to.

That's why I'm so anxious.

Because the more I think about it, the more I think I have to do it.

'What do you think?' says Gabriek.

I stare.

I think it's amazing.

It's a baby cot, beautifully built by Gabriek from bits of wood. But it's not like any baby cot I've ever seen. For a start it's on cleverly designed wooden rockers. And it's got a roof that slides shut with little wooden animals dangling from it.

'Sound-proofing,' says Gabriek. 'For when Pavlo's having a bad night.'

The cot walls and roof have lots of tiny holes drilled in them. Scientifically designed, I'm guessing, so they're small enough for air to get in but not for much sound to get out.

'Brilliant,' I say, trying not to let Gabriek see how emotional it's making me feel. And how lucky to be in a family with somebody as kind and loving as Gabriek.

I think Pavlo agrees. He's lying on his blanket in the cot, gurgling happily. Specially when Gabriek rocks him.

Suddenly I'm starting to hope it could be OK.

We're safe, the three of us, here in our hideout. We've got food and security and each other.

I'm sure a baby can survive on bread soup as long as it's got plenty of cabbage juice and mashed sardines in it.

'We need to get Pavlo a few things,' says Gabriek. 'Rubber teats for his bottle. More blankets. Little clothes for when he starts to grow. I'll have a word with some of my customers tomorrow. Get them to keep an eye out.'

I stare at Gabriek, horrified.

If he starts putting the word around that we've got a baby, sooner or later a careless customer is bound to shoot their mouth off.

And sooner or later, but probably sooner, Gogol will hear.

'What's the matter?' says Gabriek.

'We need to have a talk,' I say miserably.

'Good,' says Gabriek. 'I want to hear how you went with the doctor.'

I tell Gabriek about Gogol.

And Anya. And Doctor Lipzyk.

The paintings. Everything.

Gabriek listens silently. Grimly. Drinking a lot of vodka.

'I'm sorry,' I say miserably. 'I should have told you before.'

Gabriek doesn't reply at first. Just has another big swallow from his mug. He rubs his head, as if this is too much for one human brain to take in.

And one human heart.

'I'm sorry,' I say again.

'You did your best,' says Gabriek. 'Perhaps it might have been better if you'd found a baby somewhere else, but you didn't. And Pavlo's ours now, and that's that.'

I want to hug Gabriek.

I don't.

'Here's what we do,' says Gabriek. 'You lie low here with Pavlo. We don't need baby milk from an individual who gets kids to do his stealing for him. There's other powdered milk in this city we can get our hands on through honest black-market trading. And if this Gogol causes trouble, I'll have a word with him.'

Gabriek gets to his feet.

Unsteadily.

He goes over to his bed and reaches behind it.

I give Pavlo's cot a rock and try not to look. I know what Gabriek is doing. I wish he wasn't.

Gabriek opens his battered old suitcase.

And takes out his gun.

'When the war ended,' he says, screwing the barrel of the rifle into the wooden stock, 'I said I wouldn't kill again.'

He's having trouble getting the barrel properly fitted in. And he's slurring his words a bit.

'Well,' he says, 'looks like the war's not quite over.'

It's very late.

I can't get to sleep.

Gabriek and Pavlo are snoring peacefully in Gabriek's bed. Turns out Pavlo likes the cot to play in, but not to sleep in.

I wish I could fit into the cot myself. And pull the sound-proof lid shut and stay in there for ever.

Every time I close my eyes, I see poor Gabriek shouting a challenge to Gogol. Waving his gun. Slurring his words a bit.

I see the awful expression that dawns on poor Gabriek's face as he realises what he's up against. A ruthless, powerful, sober, cold-hearted killer. And as he realises he doesn't stand a chance.

What's that noise?

Was that from next-door's roof?

Is somebody up there?

I slip out of bed and grab my glasses and go over to the curtains and peer through a crack.

Dark shapes and shadows in the moonlight.

I stare for a long time.

I don't think it's anybody.

But will I ever be sure? Is this what it'll be like, night after night, waiting for Gogol to come and kill us?

I don't have any choice.

I have to do something.

Soon, I hope, my part in this criminal operation will be over. So I can get back to Gabriek and Pavlo. Before they wake up, if I'm lucky.

If I'm extra lucky, Gabriek won't ever find out.

But I probably won't be that lucky.

I crouch behind the bricks next to the wooden cart and peer across the street.

Dimmi and his father are leaving their apartment for their early morning visit to the food drop.

While we wait for them to go round the corner, I think about Richmal Crompton, my favourite author when I was younger. Her character William was in a gang, and they got into all sorts of trouble.

Not like this.

'They've gone,' says Vladek. 'Shall we start?'

'Wait,' says Anya.

She jumps up. Runs to the back of the building we're in. Over some rubble and out of sight.

The boys look at each other, grinning.

One of them makes a medically rude hand movement about girls needing to pee a lot.

I don't say anything, but I'm pretty sure Anya's not doing that. I think she's doing something else. As she rushed out, she had the same expression on her face as she did kneeling by the roses.

After a few minutes, she comes back, pale.

Gives me a warning glare.

'Let's go,' she says.

We sprint across the street. We're all carrying piles of bedsheets.

'If we ever do any more art thefts,' says Vladek, looking at the sheets, 'let's hope we're still living in a luxury mansion.'

I don't reply.

I won't be doing more. I'm only doing this one to get a killer off our backs. Which is why I've made sure Anya has planned it properly.

We stop and catch our breath in the foyer of the apartment building. It's one of the least-bombed foyers I've ever been in.

Anya goes over and drags the lift door open.

Is she crazy?

Lifts need electricity. The only electricity in this city is in the desk lamps of military officials. Even if you could get your hands on it, it wouldn't be enough to run a lift.

'Come on,' says Anya, and goes into the lift.

We follow, and I see something that Gabriek would be fascinated by.

If he ever speaks to me again.

Wooden steps have been cleverly built inside the lift shaft, spiralling upwards.

We climb after Anya.

Gabriek would give this ten out of ten for smart thinking.

'All this effort,' pants Bolek, 'and there's not even food up there.'

'Yeah,' says Vladek, 'but wait till you see what is up there.'

'Shhh,' whispers Anya.

On the top floor we step out of the lift shaft and stand in front of an apartment door.

I recognise the lock. It's been well fitted by someone who knows carpentry. Which is a shame. If it was badly fitted I might have been able to get the whole thing off from this side.

Instead I open my medical bag and take out the lock-picks Gabriek made.

He didn't make them for breaking in. He made them because most of the locks we salvage have lost their key, and we have to get them open so we can make a new one.

I stand close to the door and slide the two thin pieces of metal into the keyhole.

Then I close my eyes.

You have to do it by feel. It's delicate and difficult work. You have to shift the pins in the right order. It usually takes a few goes, but it's easier when you know a lock as well as I know this one.

It's also good practice. I hope one day to operate on people's insides, and I might have to close my eyes then too if I don't want to look at too much blood.

There's a click as the last pin shifts.

I open the door.

The others push past and scramble into the apartment.

I don't.

With the screwdriver I have in my bag, I take out the lodging screws from the back of the lock and prise the lock out of the door. Then I scrape and gouge the rim of the hole to make it look like the lock was ripped out.

I don't want Dimmi to know the lock was removed by somebody who knew it well.

Somebody who could only be Gabriek or me.

I put everything back in the bag, including the lock. I'd rather not steal it, but it's better if Dimmi doesn't get to examine it.

'Felix.'

I look up. Anya is coming towards me along the apartment hallway.

'Goodbye,' I say. 'I'm finished.'

'No you're not,' says Anya. 'We need your help carrying the paintings.'

I glare at her. That wasn't part of the deal.

'An extra kilo of powdered milk,' says Anya.

I think about this, then walk past her into the apartment.

A kilo is a lot of milk powder, but that's not why I'm staying. It's because of what I can see on the wall at the other end of the hallway.

A painting, an old one, of a woman and a baby. They're in a garden, leaves dappled with sunbeams. They're gazing at each other with such love the whole painting seems to shine with golden light.

There's no rubble in the picture, or sadness.

Anya stands next to me. She murmurs an Italian name, the artist's probably. I don't reply. I just want to enjoy how the painting is making me feel.

And I want to see more.

I go into the living room, which is full of boys wrapping paintings in sheets.

There are lots that haven't been wrapped yet, stacked against the walls. Dimmi and his father must have been to every bombed-out art museum in central Europe.

I go from one old painting to the next, gazing at the people in them. Their faces. Elderly people, young people. Their loving faces. It feels like being in sunlight, even though this apartment is quite dark.

I know that lots of other paintings have been done of anger and violence and war, I've seen them in books. But there are no cruel paintings here.

Even this one, for example, which shows an elderly sick man in a bed, has the patient surrounded by loving faces.

This is amazing. Here, in the middle of a wrecked city, are hundreds of years of love.

Anya thrusts a sheet into my hands.

'Get wrapping,' she says. 'We need to be out of here.'

I stare at a painting of a beautiful girl who looks a bit like Anya but without the grubby coat. She's playing with some babies in a stream. There are water lilies and animals and they're all having fun.

'Come on,' says Anya. 'Get to work.'

I take one last look at the unwrapped paintings, at what we humans can do when we have the chance to be loving and generous.

Then I throw a dusty sheet over the nearest one and get on with the work of stealing them.

Soon, I hope, Gogol will be getting a delivery that will make him so happy, he'll stick to his side of the bargain.

And not kill me and Pavlo.

So at least if Gabriek finds out I disobeyed him and ruined his reputation and wrecked his business, I can tell him the good part.

That Pavlo will be safe.

If Gogol sticks to his side of the deal.

I shiver, partly at the thought of what will happen if he doesn't, and partly because Doctor Lipzyk's hallway is so cold.

The chandelier is still here, huge and spectacular, but the candles aren't alight and its glittering crystals look hard and cruel. If it fell on you, no doctor could save you.

Come on, Anya, where are you? I want that powdered milk so I can get out of here. I want to get back to Pavlo.

Anya comes in through the front door.

'That's the penicillin on its way,' she says. 'Vladek will get it to Gogol by tonight.'

'Vladek?' I say. 'I thought Doctor Lipzyk would deliver it.'

Anya shakes her head.

'Doctor Lipzyk is busy,' she says. 'Admiring his paintings.'

I don't want to hear that. I don't want to hear that a brilliant doctor has a selfish and greedy side. Plus I don't want to hear about a gang kid with medicine worth tens of thousands of zloty in his pocket.

'What if Vladek jumps on a train to Paris?' I say.

I'm not sure if you can do that, but I don't even want him to try.

Anya gives me a weary look.

'I trust him,' she says. 'His friend Morek had typhus and Vladek stayed with him for days, even though he didn't have to, right up till Morek died.'

I nod.

'Can you get my milk now,' I say. 'I want to go.'

I can see she's hurt by how unfriendly I am.

Too bad. That's what happens in this world if you deceive people and use them.

'It'll take a few minutes,' says Anya. 'Wait in the library.'

I do. It's still an amazing library, even if it is owned by somebody who isn't quite as wonderful as I thought he was.

I run my hand along a row of beautiful books.

I could spend months in here.

Years.

But I've only got a few minutes. Last time I was here I wasted the visit collecting vomit information for someone who won't let me help her, so now I'm going to spend the time on something else.

Baby health.

Some of these books are extremely old. Which is very educational. Even hundreds of years ago, when babies looked different on the outside, they were the same on the inside as they are now.

I see some very ancient books on a top shelf. In beautiful ancient leather binding.

I go up the ladder to have a look.

Oof, heavy. You shouldn't really put books this heavy on the top shelf. Professional book people like Mum and Dad would never do that. A person could injure themselves up here just opening one.

I'm going to move these down.

First I'll clear some space on the bottom shelf.

Hang on, what's this down here? Some sort of little cupboard. It's very low down. An older person could sustain a spinal injury just trying to open it.

And this is a very big lock for a little cupboard. It's not double-action like the one on the front door. A person who knew how could crack this one.

I stare at it.

Then I do something I would never have done before today.

I push out of my head everything Mum and Dad and the nuns taught me about honesty and good manners, open my medical bag, take out the lock-picks and get to work.

I don't know exactly what I expected to find in here.

Gold, maybe. Or jewels.

Something that would help me take care of Pavlo. Something that would be only fair for me to steal from Doctor Lipzyk because he's got beautiful paintings that aren't his that are probably worth millions.

But it's just photos.

Horrible photos.

I know a doctor's work can be gruesome when it comes to blood and meat. I saw plenty of that as Doctor Zajak's assistant with the partisans. But I've never seen anything like these photos.

People walking around with their leg muscles showing.

Other people trying to pick things up with their arms half cut off.

People crying with their feet and tummies very badly burnt.

At least these poor people weren't left with their war injuries on a battlefield or a bombed-out street. These photos look like they were taken in some sort of hospital or laboratory.

And each photo has got the same word stamped on the back.

Dodoczne

I don't feel good about these photos. I shouldn't be looking at them. Only a very experienced doctor can look at photos like these without getting upset.

Quickly I put them away and lock the cupboard and put the books back in front of it and the tools back into my medical bag.

Just in time.

Anya comes in with my three kilos of powdered milk.

I put my coat on, turn my back and put the bags of milk into the inside pockets.

I nod to Anya and head to the front door.

She comes with me. I can see she's still feeling hurt by my behaviour.

What does she expect? That I'll hang around for her to come up with some other way to use me? To get something else Doctor Lipzyk wants so he'll let her stay on here?

I know using and lying is how people treat each other in the modern world, but I don't have to accept it, even if I am a thief.

I step out the door.

I should just walk away. But for some reason I think about how Mum would feel if she'd seen my behaviour today.

It's probably because of that first painting.

I can't change the things I've done, but at least I could try to be a bit more understanding of other people. And I have to admit, now I'm thinking about it, if I was sick I wouldn't want to be living on the streets either. I'd probably do just about anything to be allowed to stay.

I turn back to Anya.

'I hope you get better soon,' I say. 'Whatever it is you've got.'

She just looks at me.

For a long time.

'There's no cure,' she says, and shuts the door.

Soon, I hope, Pavlo will wake up.

Then I can get busy again. Washing him and feeding him and showing him around our hideout. Which will take my mind off things and I won't feel so worried and scared.

I could wake him up myself, but I don't want to. His little face is so peaceful while he's asleep.

So at the moment my whole mind is on things, completely on them, and I'm feeling very worried and extremely scared.

Gabriek's never done this before.

Stayed out all afternoon and half the evening.

The argument we had this morning when I got back was the worst ever. Even three kilos of powdered milk didn't calm Gabriek down.

Maybe I should have lied when he asked me where I'd been and what I'd been doing. But Gabriek and I have never lied to each other. So I told him about the art theft.

He was furious.

He opened a bottle of cabbage vodka and drank most of it.

Then he went out.

With his gun.

I'm terrified he's going to do something very dangerous. Like try to get the paintings back from Doctor Lipzyk. Who very likely has a gun himself because Anya must have picked up the habit from somewhere.

Or even worse, Gabriek might go and see Dimmi to apologise and return his lock.

Dimmi doesn't need a gun. Dimmi could tie Gabriek's gun barrel into a knot. Round Gabriek's neck.

As well as worrying about these things, I'm worrying about Anya's illness.

According to the books in Doctor Lipzyk's library, there are a lot of illnesses that cause vomiting. Some of them get better in a few days, but some of them are fatal.

What's that?

Clattering against the window?

Hail?

Can't be, it's not raining.

There it is again. Somebody's throwing stuff at our window.

Nobody knows we're here, so it must be Gabriek. So drunk he's forgotten our secret knock. Probably forgotten where the ladder's hidden too.

I hesitate. This racket could wake Pavlo. Should I slide his cot roof shut to muffle his yells?

No point with all the noise Gabriek's making.

I go over to the window and peek out. Over on next-door's roof is a figure, arms waving frantically.

The moon comes out and it's not Gabriek.

It's Anya.

I stare at her.

How does she know where we live?

No time to worry about that now because she's shouting loudly enough for the whole street to hear.

'Shhhh,' I yell.

It's the loudest noise I've ever made in this hideout.

Pavlo wakes up and starts crying. I move towards him, then turn back to the window.

What did Anya just shout?

'Felix,' she yells again. 'Let me in. It's Gabriek. He's been shot.'

I don't let her in.

I bundle Pavlo up and swing us both down on the ladder and meet her in the street.

'What happened?' I say.

'Come on,' she says.

We hurry down the street. I don't even know where we're going.

'How badly is he hurt?' I ask.

'He's alive,' says Anya. 'But he's bleeding badly. He was shot in the leg. The boys are bringing him.

But they can't move him quickly, so I came on ahead.'

'Who shot him?' I say.

I must have been wrong about Dimmi not needing a gun.

'Gogol,' says Anya.

I stumble and almost drop Pavlo. Anya reaches out to take him, but I shake my head. I'm not fainting, just sick with worry. How could anybody be shot by Gogol and still be alive?

'Are you sure he's just wounded?' I say.

Anya nods.

'Gabriek shot Gogol first,' she says. 'Wounded Gogol in the arm, that's what I heard, and Gogol fired back before his men dragged him away.'

'How do you know all this?' I say.

'I've got friends,' says Anya, giving me a look. 'Unlike some people.'

Gabriek is sprawled in the cart, the one we used for the paintings.

Vladek and Bolek and the other gang boys are wheeling him carefully towards our place.

'That's all I need,' croaks Gabriek when he sees me. 'An amateur doctor.'

He's gripping his rifle like there are still people he needs to shoot.

I can see he's still drunk. Which is just as well. I learned working with Doctor Zajak that alcohol dulls pain, and Gabriek's leg is bleeding a lot.

I give Pavlo to Anya and climb onto the cart and tear my medical bag into strips and tie them round the top of Gabriek's leg.

They slow the bleeding, but not much.

'Quick,' I say. 'He needs surgery.'

When we're close to our place, I tell the boys to stop.

'I'll take him,' I say. 'Thanks.'

I heave Gabriek off the cart. He's wobbly on his feet. But he can walk if I prop him up.

I wave the gang boys away. They understand. They know about security. They swing the cart round and head off.

'Me too?' says Anya.

I look at her. She's holding Pavlo. I can't carry him and help Gabriek.

'I'd appreciate your help,' I say.

'Only if you think about something,' she says. 'The business with the paintings. How maybe you can't see when people are trying to help you.'

Gabriek and I struggle up the ladder.

Anya follows with Pavlo.

Halfway up, while we're having a rest and I'm looking anxiously at Gabriek's leg, Gabriek sees Anya.

'She shouldn't be here,' he says. 'Why is she here?'

I've been thinking about it.

Anya didn't have to get involved in this. The friend who saw the shoot-out told her that Gogol

128

was screaming out death threats as his men carried him away. How he's going to kill Gabriek and me and Pavlo and everyone we've ever met.

Anya didn't have to put herself at risk for me again. There aren't any paintings involved this time.

I wait till we get to the top of the ladder and I have enough breath to speak. I put my mouth close to Gabriek's ear.

'She's our friend,' I say.

Soon, I hope, Anya will let me help her.

She's been very kind tonight, looking after Pavlo while I fix up Gabriek.

She helped me with the clean and heat too, which couldn't have been easy because even a huge medical library doesn't prepare you for the sight of veins and gristle after a bullet's been dug out.

'I'll bring some proper disinfectant from my place tomorrow,' she says. 'And some penicillin.'

'Thanks,' I say.

We look at each other.

Now I've got Gabriek stitched up and bandaged and he's sleeping off the vodka, we can talk.

'What is it?' I say quietly. 'Your thing that hasn't got a cure.'

I can tell from her face there's something she wants to tell me.

But she doesn't.

'It's complicated,' she says. 'We'll talk about it

another time. It's very late. I have to go.'

I want her to stay, to let me help her for once, to take a risk and trust me.

But I don't say anything.

It's probably best for her sake that she goes. I'm not a fully trained doctor yet and she's got one at her place who is.

Anyway, I've got somebody else who needs my help. And something else very important to think about.

A decision to make.

A very difficult decision.

Pavlo is asleep on my chest.

I've been lying here in bed for hours, awake.

Thinking. Making the decision. Cancelling it. Making it again.

Oh, little bundle, I wish I didn't have to do it.

But I do.

When you became my baby, I swore to keep you safe. And I thought I could. Me and Gabriek are good at hiding, so I thought you'd be safe with us.

I was wrong.

I hoped Gogol would forget about us, but he hasn't. I hoped he'd give up wanting to kill us, but he won't now, not ever.

And our security isn't working. Anya found us, and if she can, Gogol can.

I know what you'd be thinking, little bundle, if you were awake.

Why don't I go and kill Gogol to keep you safe?

I've been asking myself that all night.

Pavlo, I'm no good at killing. I'm a boy who spent two years in a hole and six months in a forest and I'm good at mending things and sometimes mending people but I'm hopeless at killing and Gogol is so good at it.

So even if I tried, you wouldn't be safe.

Which is why I have to take you away. To your people. To people who will love you and care for you.

Even though it will break my heart.

So you'll be safe.

'Ukraine?'

Gabriek blinks in the dawn light.

He groans and sinks back down onto his bed.

I can see him struggling through the pain of his leg to understand what I've just told him.

'Pavlo will be safer with his own people,' I say. 'I'm going to take him over the border into Ukraine and find a kind family who will love him and give him a home.'

Gabriek struggles up onto his elbows again.

Even in this light, which is the dullest, greyest, bleakest dawn light ever, I can see how pale he is.

'Pavlo's ours,' says Gabriek.

I feel the same.

Which is why this is so hard.

'He's not really ours,' I say. 'Not for ever. We just

borrowed him for a while to do our best for him. Which is what we still have to do.'

Gabriek looks at Pavlo, who is in his cot, sucking his toes.

What Ukrainian family wouldn't love a baby who can do that?

'I forbid you to go,' says Gabriek. 'It's too far. And too risky.'

I was worried Gabriek would say that.

'Gabriek,' I say, 'when you decided to protect me, to do your best to keep me safe, you wouldn't have let anyone talk you out of it, would you? Or let anyone make you do something you didn't think was best. Would you?'

Gabriek glares at me.

'I'd have listened,' he says. 'To someone older and wiser than me.'

I shake my head.

'No you wouldn't,' I say quietly. 'Because you'd made a vow. To me. And to your own loving heart.'

Gabriek glares at me for a long time.

Then slowly the anger leaves his face and there are just tears.

Tears happen a lot to people who drink alcohol. But not just to them, because my eyes are wet too.

Gabriek is staring at his bandaged leg. I can see that at this moment he hates his leg.

'I can't go with you,' he says.

'I know,' I say.

Gabriek hesitates.

I can see he wants to say something else.

'Felix,' he says quietly. 'You know it won't be easy, don't you?'

I nod.

But I'm more worried about Gabriek.

'We have to get you to a safe place too,' I say. 'Somewhere Gogol can't find you.'

Gabriek shakes his head.

He reaches down to the floor and picks up his gun.

'Let's agree to trust each other,' he says. 'I'll trust you to come back safely. You trust me to be here when you do.'

I can't argue with that.

'You should get started,' says Gabriek. 'Before Gogol's trigger arm starts working again.'

'Anya will be here today,' I say. 'She's bringing medical stuff for your leg. She's a bit secretive, but you can trust her too.'

Gabriek nods.

'The border's east,' he says. 'Less than a day away by train. You should be back in a few days.'

'Three,' I say.

I don't say I haven't got a clue how I'm going to get me and Pavlo onto a train. All the trains are controlled by the military authorities. I've heard they shoot people who try to jump on without a ticket.

Gabriek beckons me towards him.

I bend over his bed.

With a grimace he pulls his wedding ring off his finger and puts it into my hand.

It's gold. It's the ring that married him to Genia. It's the most precious thing he owns.

'No,' I say. 'Thanks, but it's OK. I'll manage.'

Gabriek closes my hand over the ring and holds it tight.

We look at each other. I can see he's not going to change his mind.

He gives my hand a final squeeze.

'I'm proud of you, Felix,' he says.

'Thank you,' I say.

I go over to the cot and pick Pavlo up and put him on Gabriek's chest.

I'm proud of Gabriek too. It's not easy saying goodbye when most of the people in your life have already gone.

Soon, I hope, I'll find someone who'll swap a wedding ring for a train ticket.

That's how the black market works.

I hope.

This station is more chaotic than food-drop square and the military welfare office put together.

War is a bit like blind man's buff, little bundle. Everyone ends up all over the place and they all want to get back to where they belong.

Which is what I'm trying to do for you, Pavlo.

All this noise must be scary. Come on, let's go back outside so I can give you a drink.

We push our way through the crowd, wild-eyed travellers bashing into us on all sides. I'm glad Gabriek made these new bags so strong. And I'm glad I've got Pavlo in the front bag, where I can protect him against my chest.

Outside I sit on one of the stone lions that used to be on the roof when the station had a roof.

The poor creature's lying in the street now, most of him rubble.

I take the rucksack off my back and find Pavlo's bottle and start feeding him. I do what Mum used to do to me. Hum a tune. It seems to make babies suck better.

It also stops me worrying about whether we'll get a ticket and whether we'll get on a train without being shot.

No it doesn't.

Come on, Pavlo, drink faster. We need to get back in there before the tickets run out and my plan falls in a bigger heap than this poor lion.

'Felix,' yells a voice.

You know how when somebody wants to kill you and he's on your mind the whole time and you hear somebody shouting your name and you know it's him?

Even when it doesn't sound like him?

I grab Pavlo and the rucksack and run back into the station.

'Stop,' yells the voice.

I know I shouldn't look back because it'll slow me down, but I do, just quickly, glancing over my shoulder, searching the crowd for a black leather jacket and an angry face and a gun. I don't see any of those.

I see a pink coat.

Anya hurries over, out of breath.

'I'm coming with you,' she says.

I stare at her.

'Don't argue,' she says. 'Anyway, you wouldn't make it onto the train without these.'

She's carrying a bundle. Something wrapped up in a bedsheet. Lots of things, because they clink and rattle when she moves.

'Lipzyk's best cutlery,' she says. 'He'll choke when he sees they've gone.' She gives a bitter laugh. 'It's his lucky day. Having me steal them rather than stab him with them.'

I want to ask several questions all at once, but I can't get the words out in the right order. Mostly because I've just noticed Anya's eye.

Dark and bruised and swollen.

Anya sees me looking.

'I'll tell you later,' she mutters. 'We've got a train to catch.'

The hardest part is getting to the train.

In the end we have to resort to violence.

Anya takes a fork out of her bundle and every time a person in front of us won't move, she gives him or her a little stab in the buttock.

'Don't look,' I say to Pavlo. 'We're only doing it because the world's gone mad.'

People don't like it, and a couple of them take a swipe at us, but one way or another they shift out of the way.

Then a horrible thought hits me.

'What about Gabriek?' I say, grabbing Anya's arm.

'You're meant to be looking after Gabriek.'

'Vladek's doing it,' she says, pulling away. 'He's good at looking after sick people, remember?'

I don't point out that the last time he did it, the person died. And I try not to think about what Gabriek will say when another outsider turns up at the hideout.

We finally make it to the ticket gate, and suddenly things move fast.

Anya chooses a ticket inspector with a greedy face. We have a lot of choices. The armed soldiers backing them up don't look like they spend a lot of time donating to orphanages either.

It's amazing what you can do with a couple of fistfuls of solid silver knives and forks. I've got Gabriek's ring hidden in my hand just in case, but we don't need it.

Next thing we're hurrying along the platform, trying to find a carriage that isn't already packed with people. So far they all are. Windows full of faces squashed against the glass like preserved turnips.

This carriage is crowded, but at least it's not as crowded as the train the Nazis put me on. Plus the windows are a big improvement.

And the toilet, but I don't think many of us are going to get to use it. The four or five people in there won't want to give up their space.

The train gives a lurch, but carries on chugging.

At least in this corridor we don't have to worry

about falling over. There's no room for that with so many people squashed together.

Sorry I keep wriggling, Pavlo. The straps on this rucksack are killing me.

'Why don't you take it off?' says Anya.

I give her a look. Where would I put it? The luggage racks have got soldiers sitting on them and the floor is covered with feet.

'What have you got in there, anyway?' says Anya.

I answer her without thinking.

'A folding umbrella that Gabriek invented,' I say. 'Powdered milk, water, parsnip bread, pork fat, a compass, and a bottle of cabbage vodka to give the family we find.'

Eyes flick towards us on all sides.

That was silly. I shouldn't have mentioned food and vodka out loud in here. Or a convenient way of keeping the rain off. It rains a lot where this train's going.

'Don't even think about it,' says Anya loudly.

I look at her.

She's taken a large pistol from her coat pocket.

'This gun's too big for me,' she says to the people around us. 'So if I start shooting, who knows where the bullets will go.'

Heads turn away and eyes stare at everything except my rucksack. Anya puts the gun back into her coat.

I look at her bruised eye.

She pretends not to notice, but sees that's not

working. She sighs and squeezes towards me until her lips are close to my ear.

'This morning,' she says, keeping her voice low, 'I discovered another reason why Gogol wants to kill us. The penicillin wasn't real.'

I stare at her.

'Lipzyk cheated on the deal,' she says. 'Sent Gogol fake medicine. When I found out, I went straight to Lipzyk and gave him an earful. Told him he'd put all our lives at risk, including a baby. Which must have made him feel guilty, because he lost his temper and hit me.'

Anya stares out the window.

I do too, struggling to take this in.

Gogol could have sold that penicillin to a hospital. Innocent people could have died.

I thought Doctor Lipzyk was just a brilliant doctor with an incurable dose of selfishness and greediness.

He's worse than that.

Anya has been staring out the train window for ages. Her face sometimes sad, sometimes angry.

I've been feeding Pavlo, and explaining to him why going to Ukraine is best for him.

I think it helped.

Him and me.

Now I want to help Anya.

I know usually a doctor should wait until a patient asks for treatment, it's called medical ethics.

But I'm hoping it doesn't count with friends.

I move closer to her so the other people in the train corridor won't hear.

'Anya,' I say. 'Tell me what's wrong with you, please.'

She glares at me.

I try not to think about the gun in her pocket.

'This isn't fair,' I say. 'We're in this together. You can't help me and not let me help you.'

Anya gives a loud angry sigh. Then her shoulders sag and she stares at the floor.

'You can't help me, Felix,' she says. 'What's wrong with me is I'm a bad person. I'm as bad as Lipzyk. If you knew everything about me, you'd be disgusted.'

I don't know what to say.

Tears are rolling down Anya's cheeks.

Not angry ones, sad ones.

The train slows down as it goes through a station. The name of the station slides past the window. I'm so lost in my thoughts, I don't recognise the name until we're through and picking up speed again.

Dodoczne

The word on the back of the horrible photos in Doctor Lipzyk's secret cupboard.

I don't know what Anya's done, but looking at the tears on her miserable face, I can't believe it's as bad as she thinks.

I put my hand on her arm.

'Anya,' I say. 'Sometimes we do things. All of us.'

She sniffs and wipes her eyes.

'Not you, Felix,' she says. 'You don't do bad things.'

I wish I could help her feel better. I want to give her a hug. Instead I tell her about something bad I've done. About breaking into Doctor Lipzyk's secret cupboard. About the *Dodoczne* photos.

Anya takes it all in.

Silently.

Thinking.

'I heard him use the word *Dodoczne* once,' she says. 'When I asked him about it, he told me to never mention it again.'

We both stare out the window, lost in our thoughts.

We do that all the way to Ukraine.

Except, as we discover, the train doesn't go all the way to Ukraine.

Soon, I hope, we'll be out of this cold dark forest.

And in a Ukrainian village.

Fingers crossed that Ukrainian families are more welcoming than Ukrainian forests.

'Polish trains, what a joke,' says Anya as we struggle through the wet tangled undergrowth. 'You'd think now the war's over, trains could manage to cross the border like they used to.'

'Don't worry,' I say. 'We'll be there soon.'

I hope.

A map would help. But at least I know we're heading east.

'You're incredible,' says Anya. 'Cabbage vodka and a compass.'

She gives me a grin until a wet branch slaps her in the face.

I hope Pavlo doesn't hear her swearing. It's good of her to carry him, and she's very considerate the way she takes the weight of his bag in her arms so he doesn't get too jostled. But it wouldn't be fair on a nice Ukrainian family if the first word they hear from Pavlo is a body part that only doctors should mention.

We struggle on through the forest for hours. Not much moonlight. Quite a bit of swearing.

Then suddenly we're at the edge of the trees.

In front of us, down a hill, the dark outlines of village roofs.

'Yes,' says Anya. 'At last.'

'Hold on,' I say. 'It's after midnight. If we go down there now and wake people up, they probably won't be in a very kind mood. We don't want them grumpy when they meet Pavlo. Let's have a rest and wait till daylight.'

I can see Anya doesn't think that last bit is a totally brilliant idea.

'A rest?' she says. 'Where?'

I wipe the forest drips off my glasses and peer around.

Not too far away is a big dark shape, square corners black against the night sky.

'It'll be dry and a bit warmer in that barn,' I say.

Anya stares at it suspiciously.

'We can eat in there,' I say. 'Pork fat.'

'Alright,' she says. 'But I'm checking for animals first.'

She heads towards the barn. Suddenly a beam of light slices through the darkness.

I'm about to throw myself into the mud when I remember I don't need to do that any more. There aren't Nazis any more.

The beam of light is coming from Anya.

She's got a torch.

Incredible. Only the military have torches.

I run over to her.

'Put it out,' I say. 'We don't want the locals thinking we're soldiers stealing their pigs.'

'I thought you said the locals are all asleep,' says Anya, shining the torch into the barn.

She sees it's empty and turns the torch off.

'Where did you get that?' I say.

'I took it from a Russian soldier,' says Anya.

I stare at her.

The moon comes out from behind a cloud. I can see from her face she's telling the truth.

'While he was dying,' she says.

Oh.

I wish I hadn't asked.

'See, Felix?' says Anya quietly. 'You were right. We all do things. But some of us do things that are worse.'

The pork fat was delicious and this straw is dry and warm and it feels good.

Not the prickles and the insects.

Just lying here with Pavlo and Anya.

'Shhh, little one,' I say when Pavlo starts to whimper and cry, which he does sometimes when he's been thirsty and he's drunk his milk too fast.

I wish I had some sugar water, but I don't.

Anya sits up and puts Pavlo on her shoulder. She jiggles him gently and pats his back.

'I think this is what you do,' she says.

I watch her.

One of the good things about being thirteen is that your heart is young and strong, so it can fill up with feelings like mine is now and get bigger without bursting.

Well, that's my medical opinion.

'I remember when I first saw you and Pavlo,' says Anya quietly. 'I thought to myself, I wish I was in that family.'

I look at her, surprised.

My mind starts putting things together.

Is that how Anya discovered where we live? Because she started following us?

Was that her on next-door's roof a couple of nights ago when I thought it was Gogol?

'It was just a silly dream, I knew that,' she says. 'So I carried on working hard with the gang. So I could stay in the orphanage.'

We sit in silence for a while.

'Anya,' I say. 'You were wrong before. Nothing about you would disgust me.'

I didn't plan to say that, it just came out.

Anya carefully lays Pavlo, who's asleep, on the straw.

She lies down again. So do I.

Anya doesn't say anything for a while.

'Thanks,' she says after a bit. 'But I don't think you should say that until you know the truth.'

'What is the truth?' I say.

Anya goes silent again.

I look away so she doesn't feel crowded, but I can hear her soft breathing.

'A few months ago,' she says, 'before I moved into the orphanage, I was living on the streets. Three Russian soldiers found me one night in a cellar. I was asleep. They woke me up.'

Anya pauses, then carries on.

'You're a doctor,' she says, 'so you know about soldiers in wartime. About some of them anyway. About the things they do to women.'

I nod. I do know.

'They make women have sex with them,' I say quietly. 'Or they kill the women.'

'I knew that Russian soldiers did both of those things a lot,' says Anya. 'So I knew I was in trouble. I don't speak Russian. The soldiers drew two little pictures in a notebook. To show me they were giving me a choice.'

Anya stops and breathes hard for a while. When she speaks again, her voice is a whisper, shaky with tears.

'You can guess the choice I made.'

I nod in the darkness.

My chest is hurting as I also begin to guess how she's felt since.

'Afterwards,' says Anya, 'they left me on the rubble. But I pulled myself together and followed them. They did a lot more drinking. I spent the time choosing a lump of brick. One of them went into an alley to relieve himself. I went in after him.'

She doesn't say any more. She doesn't need to. I've seen the torch.

I'm feeling so sad for her I can't speak.

I reach out to touch her arm, to let her know the only disgust I'm feeling is for grown-ups who behave like lumps of cancer.

Before I can, Anya gets up and runs to the other side of the barn and is sick. I don't blame her. I would if I was her, thinking about all this.

I go over and put my arm round her.

Gradually her body stops heaving.

I wipe her mouth with my shirt sleeve. She kneels down and starts shuddering again. This time with tears.

I kneel next to her and keep my arm round her. I remember what she said about no cure. I wish I could tell her there is, that the human heart can always be cured, but I'm just a trainee and I'm not sure.

After a while we lie down again, one on each side of Pavlo.

I slide my arm through the straw, past Pavlo's head, until I'm holding Anya's hand.

She doesn't say anything. We stay like that, not moving, not speaking, for a while.

'You're a good person, Felix,' says Anya.

Slowly she lets go of my hand and ~~rolls~~ over onto her side.

'Goodnight,' she says.

'Goodnight,' I say.

I'm glad we're in this barn.

I like barns.

In this terrible world, barns are safe.

Soon, I hope, this horrible dream will end.

Lights. Voices. Rough hands on me.

I open my eyes.

And yell.

It's not a dream.

A burning torch, blinding. My clothes undone. Men standing over me, three or four, pointing, faces twisted with hatred, shouting.

In another language, but one word I recognise. I know it in several languages. You have to.

'Jew.'

They're staring at my private part.

One of the men swings at my head with a scythe I roll to one side. The blow misses. The sharp blade jams into the dirt floor.

I kick out at the man. All the men.

'Stop it,' screams a voice.

The men freeze.

Anya is on her feet, aiming her gun at them.

I grab Pavlo, who is howling. Get him far away from the men. To the back of the barn.

Anya is screaming at the men. They start moving towards her.

She shoots one.

He falls and the others back off.

I look around wildly. Rotting planks at the back of the barn. I kick them and my leg crashes through. I kick more. And again.

'Anya,' I yell.

She glances round, still pointing the gun at the men.

Backs towards me.

'You first,' I yell at her.

The men are starting to advance.

'Give me the gun,' I say to her. 'You take Pavlo. I'll hold them off.'

The men rush us.

Anya shoots another one.

I clasp Pavlo tight and grab Anya with my other hand and crash us all through the hole except there's nothing on the other side and we're falling in blackness and I don't have Pavlo any more.

My arms are empty.

'Pavlo!' I scream.

Icy water. Smashing into it. Under. Up with a desperate yell. Anya flailing next to me. Fast water sweeping us away.

Empty arms.

'Pavlo,' I scream again.

Fast water. In my throat. Drowning my screams. Drowning my sobs.

Empty arms.

Nothing.

I open my eyes.

Daylight.

My head hurts.

It's my glasses. They're still wedged painfully on my face. Gabriek is always telling me to take them off before I lie down.

Where am I?

Mud. I'm lying on cold wet mud. Shivering. Everything's cold and wet. My feet are in a river. Just shallow water, so that's alright.

No it's not. Next to me on the mud is a sodden pink coat.

'Anya,' I croak. 'Pavlo.'

Please.

Please let them be alive.

Both of them cuddling on the mud together, waiting for me to find them.

While I struggle to my feet, I think about Anya and all the things she's done for me.

Rescued me.

Protected me.

Even though, when she needed those things herself, there was nobody to rescue and protect her.

I make a vow.

If they're still alive, I will never leave them again. I will give them good protection.

For ever.

'Felix.'

Anya's voice, calling.

I turn round.

She's walking slowly towards me through the reeds. Stumbling in the shallow water.

Crying.

Carrying a tiny sodden bundle.

Soon, I hope …
No I don't.
What's the point.

We stop walking when we get to the forest.

There are voices and dogs in the distance, but I don't care. Neither does Anya.

We kneel in the mud and dig with our hands.

Before we put Pavlo into the earth, we do what we can for his little body. Carefully pick the gravel out of his skin from his journey down the river. Gently remove the silt from his mouth.

Then Anya and I wrap Pavlo in his blanket and lay him in his little grave.

'I'm sorry,' I whisper to him.

Anya does too.

Slowly, handful by handful, we say goodbye.

* * *

We don't say anything to each other.

We haven't got the words.

Some stories don't need words. You know some stories in your heart.

You know you did your best and it wasn't enough.

You know you had hope for the world and it wasn't enough either.

I'm sitting with my back against a tree, cold wet grey forest all around. There's nowhere else to go.

I'm not sure where Anya is. I can't hear her so maybe she's gone back to Poland. It doesn't matter. She's better off without me. No vow I make will be enough to protect her.

I close my eyes.

This is what hurts most about being a human.

Doesn't matter how big your heart is, or how high your hopes are, or how far you go to try to make things right, in this world it's never enough.

'Felix.'

I wipe my eyes.

Anya is kneeling next to me.

'Felix, I need your help,' she says.

I try to explain to her that I'm the wrong person. I remind her what happened to the last person who needed my help. We still have some of his grave under our fingernails.

'There's another baby,' says Anya.

I look at her.

I don't understand.

She places my hand on the damp wool of her jumper.

On her belly.

I stare at her.

She nods.

I read in Doctor Lipzyk's library how being pregnant is one of the things that make women throw up, but I had no idea . . .

I struggle to find the words.

'The Russian soldiers?'

Anya nods again. 'I found out a few weeks ago,' she says. 'It's why I moved into the orphanage. So I'd have a doctor around.'

'Did he know?' I say. 'That you're having a baby?'

Anya shakes her head.

'Lipzyk thought I was just swapping gang chores for food and a room,' she says. 'Until yesterday. He must have guessed. He asked me and I told him.'

'And he still hit you,' I say.

'I hit him first,' says Anya. 'After he told me he didn't want trash in his house.'

I can see her doing it.

'You did the right thing, leaving,' I say. 'Your baby will have a better life away from that place.'

'That's what I was thinking until yesterday,' says Anya. 'But after what happened last night, I can't take the risk. My baby will be half Russian. Most of Europe hates Russians now. At least at Lipzyk's house my baby will be safe and well fed.'

She's looking at me pleadingly.

'I need to get back as quickly as possible,' she says. 'To say sorry. To ask his forgiveness. Will you help me?'

There's so much I want to say. About the Anya I once knew. Who didn't ask pustules like Doctor Lipzyk for their forgiveness. Who stuck a gun in their mouth instead.

But I don't.

We do what we have to do to survive.

I have to stop pretending we can make things better. We can't. The world is what it is. That couldn't be clearer. Just look around.

I made a vow to protect Anya, but I can't.

Maybe Doctor Lipzyk can.

'Yes,' I say. 'I'll help you go back.'

Soon, I hope, I'll get used to it this way.

Not getting involved in other people's business.

Not taking unnecessary risks.

Accepting the world the way it is and probably always has been.

Look how much easier it is. Here we are, back on the train, heading for home. All it took was a handful of slightly battered silver knives and forks from Anya's coat pockets. Once she'd brushed the river silt off them, the ticket inspector couldn't have been more helpful. Even though we're a bit damp and muddy.

We even got seats.

Much easier this way.

So why can't I accept that? Why am I sitting here about to explode?

Simple.

Anya is going back to a man who has no kindness in his soul or any of his major organs.

Which medically and scientifically speaking is something a person should only do once they've had a chance to examine all the information.

I lean across and whisper to Anya.

'We need to stop the train at the next station,' I say.

'We can't,' she says. 'It's an express.'

'We need to,' I say. 'Can you cause a fuss as we come into the station so I can pull the emergency cord without being seen?'

Anya thinks about this.

She looks at me again, and she must see how important this is, because she gives a nod.

We're coming into the station now.

We've just passed the first sign.

Dodoczne.

I glance at Anya. Our eyes meet.

She lets out a shriek and throws herself against the passengers next to her.

'Oh God,' she yells. 'I'm having a baby. Help me, I'm having a baby.'

The whole carriage stares at her, and a couple of people push towards her to try to help.

While everyone's attention is on her, I stand up and pull the cord.

With a hiss of brakes, the train lurches to a stop.

As I'd hoped, the train engineers are doing an inspection of every carriage. I know a bit about trains. In the war, Gabriek used to blow them up.

Passengers are happily stretching their legs on the platform.

Including the passengers from our carriage, who calmed down when I explained to them that Anya isn't having her baby for months yet, but she gets a bit emotional when she thinks about the responsibilities ahead.

'Come on,' I say to her.

We go down the platform to the ticket office.

In the cubicle is an elderly man.

'Excuse me,' I say to him. 'Can I ask you something about this district?'

The ticket man gives me a look as if that's the question he'd least like to be asked in the whole world. As if, 'do you have any pimples on your bottom and can we see them?' would be preferable.

I carry on anyway.

'Is there a hospital around here?' I ask. 'Or some other kind of medical building?'

The man's eyes narrow.

'Are you being funny?' he says.

'No,' I say, confused.

Me and the man look at each other.

'You don't know, do you?' he says.

'No,' says Anya crossly. 'That's why he asked.'

'Not a hospital,' says the man. 'A Nazi laboratory. Where Nazi doctors did experiments on people who weren't even sick. Cut them open while they were still alive. There, that's more than you wanted to know, eh?'

Actually, it's exactly what I wanted to know.

'Did a Doctor Lipzyk work there?' I ask.

Out of the corner of my eye I can see Anya frowning. She's right, it is probably a crazy thing to ask. But sometimes you have to anyway.

'No idea,' says the man. 'But they were all Nazis. Lipzyk sounds like a Polish name.'

Anya and I glance at each other. She's looking relieved. And it is possible that Doctor Lipzyk is interested in the work the Nazis did at Dodoczne for purely scientific reasons.

'The chief medical officer up there was called Hermann Lederhaus,' says the ticket man. 'They never caught him. May he rot in hell with his leg muscles flapping.'

'What did he look like?' I ask.

That's worth asking too. Even though I've read how people can have their faces changed surgically if they have good medical connections.

'Never met him,' says the ticket man. 'You had to be Jewish to have that pleasure.'

Back on the train, we stay standing.

We're exhausted and we'd like to sit. A few kind people offer their seats to Anya. But we say no. If we stand here in the corridor with our heads close together, we can talk in private.

I tell Anya the thought I had in the ticket office. About people getting their face changed if they have good medical connections.

I've just remembered the man with the very bandaged head outside Doctor Lipzyk's house. *Those bandages need to be out of sight*, that's what Lipzyk said to him.

'What if Lipzyk is a Nazi,' I say,' but he's decided he doesn't need to get his face changed? Because all the people he worked on in the laboratory are dead. And now everyone thinks he's a respectable Polish doctor running an orphanage. But he still helps his Nazi friends by changing their faces.'

Anya thinks about this.

She looks doubtful.

'I did see a couple of patients in the house,' she says. 'And they did have bandaged faces. But half the population of Europe have got war-damaged faces. Patients with bandaged faces don't make a doctor a Nazi. Nor do a few photos.'

We stare out of the train window for a while.

'We need proof,' I say.

'Risky,' says Anya. 'If we're wrong, me and my baby are out on the street.'

And if we're right, I tell her, she and her baby are in serious danger. It wasn't just Jewish people the Nazis hated, they hated Slavic people as well. Lots of Russians are Slavic. If a Nazi discovers he's got a Slavic baby in his house . . .

Anya nods. She knows all this.

For a fleeting moment I want to tell her to forget Lipzyk. To come and live with me and Gabriek.

Then I remember Gogol.

163

Anya and her baby wouldn't be any safer with us.

If he chooses, Lipzyk can make her child very safe and very comfortable. Whether or not he's a Nazi. In a world where very few babies have either of those things.

So this is Anya's decision. I don't pressure her with my feelings about Lipzyk. That if he's a Nazi I want him to die.

'OK,' says Anya after staring out the window for a long time. 'Let's do it. Let's find out for sure about Lipzyk. It's what a good mother would do, right?'

'I think so,' I say.

Anya takes a deep breath.

'Scary,' she says.

'Probably best if we have some insurance,' I say.

Anya looks at me.

'Insurance?' she says.

'I suggest Dimmi,' I say.

Soon, I hope, I'll find what I'm looking for.

I close the door behind me and immediately I wish Doctor Lipzyk's library wasn't so big. My heart valves are knotted with anxiety. Too many shelves and not enough time.

I do some slow breathing and listen carefully.

No sounds of shouting or violence from anywhere in the house.

Anya must be doing a good job. Telling Doctor Lipzyk the story we made up about our trip to Ukraine. How the purpose of it was to find a barn we'd heard about that's full of precious old hidden paintings. Which we can bring back for Doctor Lipzyk if he wants them.

It's not a true story, but with a bit of luck it's good enough to give me time.

To do my medical research.

To find the scientific evidence we need.

I start hunting for Doctor Lipzyk's real name.

People often write their names in their books. Mum and Dad were always complaining about it when they bought second-hand books for their shop.

If Doctor Lipzyk used to have a different name, perhaps he wrote it in his books back then.

OK, it's a long shot, but some of the greatest scientific discoveries in medical history have been long shots.

As I look, book by book, shelf by shelf, I listen anxiously.

Still no shouting.

What's this? A German name?

No, it's the name of a university.

I search the whole room. Every shelf.

Nothing.

A few books have a small part of the first page cut away, which could be suspicious. But it might not. The books might be second-hand. Mum and Dad used to cut the names out of their second-hand books.

Then I have a thought. Maybe I don't need to find his real name written down. Maybe there's another way.

I haven't got my lock-picks any more, so I use two thin pieces of metal I snap off an ashtray on the desk to open the secret cupboard. I take out the *Dodoczne* photos and study each one closely. This is the second time I've looked at them, but it's still very upsetting.

I stick at it. Anya's safety depends on it. These photos are a reminder of how much danger she and her baby could face in this house. Not all the poor people being mutilated in the laboratory are Jewish. Some of them look Russian.

Photo after photo after horrible photo.

And then, yes, there it is.

In the background of a terrible photograph of a poor man trying to swim with no legs.

A blurred figure in a Nazi uniform.

But not that blurred.

Doctor Lipzyk.

He's in three of the photographs.

I have to move fast.

I put them inside my shirt, run out of the house and peer down the street. In the distance are two figures. I can't see if they're the people I want them to be, so I just have to hope they are.

No time to hang around to be sure. I don't want to leave Anya on her own with Doctor Lipzyk. Not now I know who he really is.

I pin one of the photos to the outside of the front door with a couple of rose thorns. Then I hurry back inside and down the hallway until I hear Anya and Doctor Lipzyk's voices coming from a room.

The door is open just a crack.

I pause.

I want to go in and grab Doctor Lipzyk and tell him I know what he's done. Then I want to kill him.

For Mum and Dad and Zelda and all the others.

But I don't.

Not yet.

I peek into the room. Anya and Doctor Lipzyk are sitting at a table in front of a fire. The room is a bit like the library, but it's not a book room. The walls are covered with paintings. Paintings of love. Paintings of tender human goodness.

Dimmi's paintings.

'I've listened to you enough,' Doctor Lipzyk is saying to Anya. 'No more. You disgust me, young lady. You disgust me with your polluted body and you disgust me with your silly stories and lies.'

Anya is scowling. But underneath I can see how scared she is.

I go in.

'Felix,' says Doctor Lipzyk.

His mouth smiles but his eyes are like the crystal in his chandeliers.

It can't be easy for him, having a Jewish vermin and a future Slavic baby inside his house at the same time.

'Hot chocolate?' he asks.

'No thanks,' I say.

'Of course not,' says Doctor Lipzyk. 'You're a clever boy, Felix. You know that a doctor like me can give you something much better than hot chocolate.'

He gets up, opens a big black leather medical bag and takes out a syringe. The syringe has a long needle and yellow liquid inside it.

'The world is a broken and miserable place,' says Doctor Lipzyk. 'Disease all around us. In this syringe is what's called a vaccination. One little jab, and both of you will be free of disease for ever.'

I glance at Anya. She looks like she's thinking the same as me.

For Doctor Lipzyk, we're the disease. So whatever is in that syringe definitely isn't good protection.

We could try to grab it from him, but one little jab and Doctor Lipzyk would be free of us for ever.

I can see Anya is wishing her gun wasn't in a river in Ukraine.

Doctor Lipzyk goes over to the door and locks it.

'Just a little precaution,' he says, coming towards us. 'Every doctor knows how much children hate needles.'

I try to hear if there are any voices outside in the hallway.

None.

We need something to distract him. Something to take his mind off killing us, just for a couple of minutes.

From inside my shirt I take one of the photos. My hands are trembling as I put it on the table.

Face down. Better not to rush things.

'What's this?' says Doctor Lipzyk.

We all look at it. On the back of it we can see the word *Dodoczne*.

'We've just been there,' says Anya.

Doctor Lipzyk's eyes narrow very slightly.

'So?' he says.

I turn the photograph over.

Anya gasps.

We look at Doctor Lipzyk in his Nazi uniform, standing very close to the man swimming in agony.

Doctor Lipzyk tightens his grip on the syringe.

'A photo,' he says. 'A photo proves nothing. It doesn't begin to tell the whole story.'

I put another *Dodoczne* photo, another horrible part of Doctor Lipzyk's story, onto the table.

Doctor Lipzyk doesn't even look at it.

'You children,' he hisses. 'You couldn't possibly know the opportunities such a unique time gave to medical science. The discoveries that were made that will benefit humankind for ever.'

Suddenly from the front garden I hear Dimmi swearing and threatening to do medical damage to something and Bolek trying to bring him into the house.

Doctor Lipzyk grabs Anya.

She struggles to get away from him.

'Call yourself a doctor,' she spits at him. 'Felix has got more doctor in his little finger than you've got in your whole carcass.'

Doctor Lipzyk raises the syringe. He's going to plunge it straight through Anya's jumper.

I throw myself at him.

He kicks me in the legs.

I collapse, my eyes squeezed shut with the pain.

But my ears are still working. From the hallway I hear an explosion of cursing and thumping.

'Murdering Nazi vermin,' roars an angry voice, and as my eyes clear, Dimmi smashes through the door like a convoy of trucks.

There weren't just paintings in Dimmi's flat. There was a photo with a very sad inscription on the frame. Dimmi's Jewish mother, killed by the Nazis.

Dimmi's hands clamp round Doctor Lipzyk's throat. Doctor Lipzyk's feet leave the carpet. And don't come back down until the doctor finally chokes out an answer to the question Dimmi keeps yelling at him.

'Lederhaus,' croaks the doctor, his face the colour of blood. 'If you know the answer, why are you putting me through this. I'm Doctor Hermann Lederhaus.'

Anya is staring at him like she's going to be sick.

Doctor Lederhaus gets his breath back and sneers at her.

'I can see what you're thinking,' he says. 'Well, I'm not the only liar here, am I, young lady? And if your child finds out everything you've done, who'll be the monster then?'

Dimmi heaves Doctor Lederhaus into the air again until all that comes out of his throat is a gurgle.

But the damage is done. I can see on Anya's face what she's feeling.

She rushes out of the room.

I start to go after her, then stop.

Doctor Lederhaus's face, with Dimmi's hands still round his neck, is turning blue. In another minute he'll be dead.

I should be glad.

But suddenly I'm not.

Because if Mum and Dad and Zelda and Barney and Genia were still alive, I don't think they'd want the world to be like it is now. Full of people still trying to solve every problem by killing each other. I think they'd want something better.

I grab one of the paintings off the wall. It's the one of the mother and child. I hold it in front of Dimmi's face.

His furious eyes focus on it.

He recognises it.

He drops the unconscious Doctor Lederhaus onto the carpet and hugs the painting to his chest lovingly.

Anya stands in the hallway, under the chandelier, sobbing.

I go to her and put my arms round her. She doesn't move away.

We stay silent.

I want to tell her how nothing that happened to her was her fault. That none of it will stop her being a good parent. But I'm only thirteen and it's not for me to say.

It's for her to say.

She puts her arms round me and we hold each other for a long time.

'Thank you,' she whispers.

Above us a hundred candles burn brightly.

I think of them as birthday candles for the child inside Anya.

A hundred happy birthdays.

With a bit of luck. And help.

Now that's worth hoping for.

Soon, I hope, we can untie Doctor Lederhaus.

He's struggling so much, I'm worried about the medical state of his wrists and ankles. Much more of this and they'll be as chafed as his throat.

I'm also worried about his heart and lungs and spleen. Dimmi and I are keeping our feelings under control, but I can't say what'll happen once Dimmi finishes stacking his paintings.

Come on, Anya. Hurry back with the officials who put Nazis into small rooms.

Here's someone arriving now.

It's not Anya, it's Bolek and the other gang boys with the cart to transport Dimmi's paintings.

Hang on, there's somebody in the back of the cart.

It's Vladek.

I hurry outside.

Vladek is lying in the cart, barely conscious. Bleeding and battered.

'What happened?' I say, a horrible fear about Gabriek starting to grow inside me.

The other boys swap concerned glances.

'It's not good news, Felix,' says Bolek. 'Gogol picked up Vladek a couple of hours ago. He beat it out of him.'

'I'm sorry,' whispers Vladek.

'Beat what out of him?' I say, panic rising.

'Your address,' says Bolek.

I run.

Rubble doesn't stop me, crowds don't stop me, painful legs don't stop me, rising terror squeezing all the air from my chest doesn't stop me.

Please, not Gabriek.

I can survive anything else, but not Gabriek.

No security precautions this trip. No fast turns. No point.

I should probably slow down as I get close to our place. Gogol could be waiting for me. I could be in the sights of his gun right now.

I don't slow down.

I crash into our ground-floor entrance.

And stop. The ladder is out. But something's not right. It's hanging at a strange angle, away from the wall.

Then I see something even worse.

Half of it is on the ground, twisted and broken.

Oh.

Someone is lying under it, also twisted and broken.

And stiff and dead. Looking like they've fallen at least one, maybe two storeys.

It's Gogol.

Gabriek is waiting for me at the top. I scramble up the wall and the rest of the broken ladder like a demented monkey. One who can put up with any amount of leg pain.

I hug Gabriek for ages.

Then I look back down at Gogol's twisted body.

'What happened?' I say.

'Terrible accident,' says Gabriek. 'Ladder broke. Very shoddy workmanship.'

I stare at him.

Gabriek sits on his bed with a wince. His leg looks like it's been bleeding through the bandage. I'll have to fix that.

Then I see what's lying on the bed next to him.

His gun.

And something else.

Two of the securing bolts from the ladder. Which I know were installed properly. I helped Gabriek do it.

I look at him. Our eyes meet briefly. I catch a very quick twinkle before he looks away. Back down at Gogol's body.

'Oh, and I might have to give up vodka,' says Gabriek. 'Been another tragic accident. Distilling equipment's broken.'

I can see it is. It's lying next to Gogol in pieces.

Some of it seems to have blood on it, as if it was dropped onto Gogol from a great height.

Well, two storeys.

Gabriek puts his arm round me.

'Well done both of us for sticking to our agreement,' he says. 'Both here safe and sound.'

Over Gabriek's shoulder, I see Pavlo's cot.

And suddenly I can't keep the sadness in any more.

'Oh, Gabriek,' I sob.

Gabriek can't either when I tell him.

We hold each other.

Sometimes in life it's all you can do.

Wait for the sadness to be over. Hope one day it will be.

Soon, I hope, this is what will happen.

People will start to get better.

The city will start to heal.

Me and Gabriek and Anya and her baby will live together in our hideout, safe and happy behind our sack curtains.

A family.

With a very fine cot.

And nearly a thousand medical books. Which will only be fair, when you think of all the books the Nazis took from Mum and Dad.

Anya and I will further our education. We'll read a lot and get lots of medical experience in food-drop square.

Gabriek will do good work for our customers, and babysit, drunk with baby love.

And in the evenings, when Anya and I walk together among the moonlit rubble heaps, I'll slip my arm through hers and our hearts will be full.

This is what I hope will happen.
And I think it will.
Soon.

Dear Reader

So far there are five in this family of books.

In Once, Then, After and Soon, we share Felix's early years as he struggles to keep his friends and optimism alive through World War Two and what follows.

Between writing Then and After, I wanted to find out how Felix's childhood experiences, in particular the terrible years of the Holocaust, would shape his adult life. So I wrote Now, in which the 80-year-old Felix is still battling and still optimistic, and finally happy.

There are two reasons I call this a family of books. The first is that years ago, when I started my work with Felix, I quickly came to see him and his friends and the brave adults who look after them as just that, a family.

The other reason I prefer not to call these books a series is that I've tried to write them so they can be read in any order. Most of us prefer reading to queuing, and sometimes we can't choose when we get our hands on a book.

If Soon is your first encounter with Felix, please don't be perturbed. You now know a few things about Felix's earlier years, but not enough to spoil the other stories.

For their help with the publishing, research, editing, design, marketing and distribution of Soon, my heartfelt thanks to Laura Harris, Kathy Toohey, Heather Curdie, Tony Palmer, Tina Gumnior and Kristin Gill. And my warm appreciation to the other wonderful Penguins in Australia and the UK, and to the non-avians at publishing houses in other countries. Thank you all.

Felix's stories come from my imagination, but also from a period of history that was all too real. I couldn't have written any of them without first reading many books about the Holocaust and what came after – books that are full of the real voices of the people who lived and struggled and loved and faced death in that terrible time.

You can find details of some of my research reading on my website. I hope you get to delve into some of those books and help keep alive the memory of those people.

This story is my imagination trying to grasp the unimaginable. Their stories are the real stories.

Morris Gleitzman
April 2015

www.morrisgleitzman.com

MORRIS GLEITZMAN

Everybody
deserves
to have
something good in their life.

At least

Once.

Once I escaped from an orphanage to find Mum and Dad.
Once I saved a girl called Zelda from a burning house.
Once I made a Nazi with toothache laugh.
My name is Felix.
This is my story.

'... moving, haunting and funny in almost equal measure,
and always gripping ...' *Guardian*

'This is one of the most profoundly moving novels
I have ever read. Gleitzman at his very best has created one
of the most tender, endearing characters ever to grace the
pages of a book.' *Sunday Tasmanian*

'... a story of courage, survival and friendship told
with humour from a child's view of the world.'
West Australian

I had a plan for me and Zelda.
Pretend to be someone else.
Find new parents.
Be safe for ever.
Then the Nazis came.

'... an exquisitely told, unflinching and courageous novel.'
Age

'[Gleitzman] has accomplished something extraordinary,
presenting the best and the worst of humanity without stripping
his characters of dignity or his readers of hope.'
Guardian

'Gleitzman's Felix and Zelda are two of the finest and
sure-to-endure characters created in recent times.'
Hobart Mercury

After the Nazis took my parents I was scared.
After they killed my best friend I was angry.
After they ruined my thirteenth birthday I was determined.
To get to the forest.
To join forces with Gabriek and Yuli.
To be a family.
To defeat the Nazis after all.

Sometimes facing the past is the bravest act of all . . .

Once I didn't know about my grandfather Felix's scary childhood.
Then I found out what the Nazis did to his best friend Zelda.
Now I understand why Felix does the things he does.
At least he's got me.
My name is Zelda too.
This is our story.

'*Now* is an edifying and tender, nuanced novel from
an exceptionally compassionate author.'
Age

'Gleitzman has a special way of seeing the world through the eyes
of a child, and generations of readers are grateful to him for it.'
West Australian

'Gleitzman's trademark fine balance of tragedy and
comedy is as sure as ever.'
Guardian

It all started with a Scarecrow

Puffin is over seventy years old.
Sounds ancient, doesn't it? But Puffin has never been
so lively. We're always on the lookout for the next big
idea, which is how it began all those years ago.

Penguin Books was a big idea from the mind of
a man called Allen Lane, who in 1935 invented
the quality paperback and changed the world.
**And from great Penguins, great Puffins grew,
changing the face of children's books forever.**

The first four Puffin Picture Books were hatched in 1940 and the
first Puffin story book featured a man with broomstick arms called
Worzel Gummidge. In 1967 Kaye Webb, Puffin Editor, started the
Puffin Club, promising to **'make children into readers'**.
She kept that promise and over 200,000 children became devoted
Puffineers through their quarterly instalments of *Puffin Post*.

Many years from now, we hope you'll look back and
remember Puffin with a smile. **No matter what your age
or what you're into, there's a Puffin for everyone.**
The possibilities are endless, but one thing is for sure:
whether it's a picture book or a paperback, a sticker book
or a hardback, **if it's got that little Puffin
on it – it's bound to be good.**

www.puffinbooks.com